MW01521031

SEARCHING FOR HULA LOVE
UNDER A BLUE PAPAYA MOON

SEARCHING FOR HULA LOVE UNDER A BLUE PAPAYA MOON

SHORT STORIES about the yearning in all blue-collar dreaming to bring back the impossible hopes of our youth and to find a way to outlive the devil—Some true, some not so true, but all written with a smile by America's number one fun motivator...

Bob Basso

iUniverse, Inc.

New York Lincoln Shanghai

Searching For Hula Love Under A Blue Papaya Moon

All Rights Reserved © 2004 by Robert L. Basso

No part of this book may be reproduced or transmitted in any form or by any means, graphic, electronic, or mechanical, including photocopying, recording, taping, or by any information storage retrieval system, without the written permission of the publisher.

iUniverse, Inc.

For information address:
iUniverse, Inc.
2021 Pine Lake Road, Suite 100
Lincoln, NE 68512
www.iuniverse.com

ISBN: 0-595-33557-8

Printed in the United States of America

C O N T E N T S

▼

PREFACE

Some of these stories are verbatim true, others more or less true but all contain some truth. I've always believed fiction is nothing more than non-fiction with more adjectives.

We see the world the way we need to see it, not the way it is, and that's a good thing for authors; otherwise we'd all be National Geographic photographers and plumbing contractors.

To tell you the downright truth, I don't remember which ones are real and which ones are imagined. Maybe it doesn't matter. Maybe we'll all live long enough to discover the final wisdom is that everything under the stars—jacaranda trees, day-glo tank tops, creativity, the human genome, and fantasy itself are all equal elements of the same plot line.

I do remember that somehow my strange, funny, improvised life passed through each of these stories in a conscious way.

I wrote them down for the same reason old men chase young women and middle-aged men leave their wives for nineteen year old dental assistants: we're afraid to die and we need hope that by starting a new story we've gained a reprieve to continue on for a few more chapters of life.

I can't believe any of what I just said is even remotely profound or titillating enough to want to make you explore the pages within, but, then again, this is only a preface. What can you expect?

If you're still searching for a reason to continue, consider this consolation: there is no credible evidence that anyone ever died while reading a book of short stories.

Bob Basso

P.S. Please find a way to enjoy the stories marked "Unedited." It'll drive my publisher nuts and give me a small but significant pleasure. I've always believed entries in a diary are more self-revelatory than all the thick bound volumes of autobiographies combined.

Most published writing is polished rewriting, hardly spontaneous, rarely capturing truth in motion, unaware. So I prevailed upon my steely disciplined editors, who predict instant doom and forgettable oblivion for my literary exploits, to allow me to include stories written in one sitting as they gushed through my senses into my two typing fingers. No rewrite; no vanity polishing, like life itself. Why not? After all, reality never unfurls so neatly as it does in the middle of the structured syntax of a novel, but rather it hurls itself at us as a garbled rush of short stories, a burst of something unexpected that carries us to unguarded moments we never planned and for which we have no ending.

I think I've just impressed myself with all this explanation, but, then again, it may all be nothing more than a wordy disclaimer for poor grammar. I apologize to you, the reader, and especially to Sister Mary Alphonse, my long-suffering second grade teacher.

THE MEANING OF LIFE

Author's note: Don A, holistic guru and the editor of one of the largest wellness magazines called, "Bob, I'm running a series on the MOL (that's insider shorthand for the Meaning of Life), and want you to be one of the one hundred wellness leaders to give us your answer."
I was flattered and humbled to think I was being included in such a robust corps of healers. Like all great teachers, their illuminating responses filled the reader with hope and a need to rediscover the history of philosophy. I have no idea why my pedestrian fluff was chosen to be the first one featured, but it seems appropriate to begin this anthology of stories searching for the same answer.

For fifty years I've had daily conversations with God. We talk about everything—why bad things happen to good people, why the good die young, and why He let the Dodgers leave Brooklyn and break my heart forever. I've asked Him a thousand times, "What is the MOL," and a thousand times the answer comes back the same, "Ask your mother!" I rarely agree with God on anything, but I knew this was His best suggestion yet. Mothers are the only truly wise people on the planet, because they are the only ones chosen to work with God (or whatever you call the ultimate force) in creating life. So on July 31, 1987, at one o'clock in the morning on the lanai of her Waikiki condo, as my father lay dying in the next room, I asked her. She took a deep breath, looked up at a full moon hanging low over Diamond Head, and said, "Stop wrestling with mysteries. Know what you know. Don't hurt anybody, and be good to yourself." She paused, then added, "Eat plenty of fruit."

My universe has been clear ever since.

THE LEGEND OF
MONSIEUR
BEAUMARCHAISE

The TVG high-speed train from La Baule to Paris was right on time—twenty minutes late. The thirty or so commuters standing in the perpetual May drizzle remained stolid and unphased at the expected announcement. This was Bretagne, western France, inhabited by the Alpine race, hearty red-cheeked farm types who still held on to their stoic ancestral Celtic and Nordic codes. They had withstood five hundred years of foreign invasion including the latest, and to many the most deadly, from the dreaded Parisian resort developers seeking to colonize the six miles of Atlantic beaches where once mystical Druids, the diabolic Richelieu, and a long line of Louies played. A twenty-minute delay just wasn't worth a centime of concern.

I was waiting for Monsieur Beaumarchaise. He was sure to be on it or would certainly board in Pornichet, St. Nazaire, or Nantes, the only stops on the three-and-a-half hour run to Gar du Montparnasse, the southernmost railway hub in Paris.

I had no idea who Monsieur Beaumarchaise was or what he looked like or what significance, if any, he represented in the life of Bretons, but meeting him was becoming the overwhelming obsession of my life. All I knew was that the mere mention of his name brought an amazing shift in body chemistry. An instant sunshine. The sullen waitress at La Flambee Craperie immediately broke her mask of ennui with a smile when she noticed my train tickets on the table.

"Ah, you are on the train from La Baule to Paris. Be sure to watch out for Monsieur Beaumarchaise."

In my best broken French. I inquired, "And who might this cause celebre be? Movie star, local hero, footballer, renowned thinker. Who?"

With a slight hint of Gaulish arrogance, she replied, "Oh, monsieur, he is much more than that. You will surely know that when you see him."

More than a movie star, hero, or great thinker? My God, Napoleon, Moliere and deGaulle were long gone. What other great sons of the Republique were left? How gargantuan can this living myth be?

After three months of roaming every cobbled square and gray stone village on the coast searching the history of western France in World War II, I felt I had absorbed as much insight into this land and its people as de Tocqueville had about my country in his celebrated observations. Obviously, Mr. Beaumarchaise was a creature of modern times and had escaped my consistent look backward.

I had learned enough of the French sensibility not to press my ignorance further, at least with Mademoiselle Sullen.

The frozen grin on the station master's face suddenly got wider as I again probed for answers.

"Do you suppose Monsieur Beaumarchaise will be on this train?"

"Oui, monsieur, indubitablement. At some point he will board. He always does." Before I could press the issue further, he had crossed the tracks to the westbound side to move a baggage cart in place for the approaching 227 from Rennes.

At precisely twenty minutes past the hour, the muffled sound of a train whistle broke through the rain and fog at the far end of the platform. Like a sleek silver-backed whale breaching suddenly from another world, the 557 was upon us. From across the tracks, Monsieur Frozen Grin shouted, "La Baule a Paree. La Baule a Paree." Twenty-nine commuters dutifully lined up on the numbers imprinted on the ground corresponding to their car number and quietly without incident or annoyance embarked.

I thoroughly enjoyed the patient civility and waited behind to take it all in. It also gave me an excellent opportunity to see if any likely candidates for national adoration disembarked. None did. Beaumarchaise was either onboard or soon would be.

I found my second-class window seat in the non-smoking kiosk right behind the locomotive, an excellent vantage point to see who got on and off at the next three stops before Paris.

A quick inspection of my six fellow non-smokers revealed two tall, chatty blond German backpackers, a very bent old lady in black with Ben Franklin eye-glasses, a bright-eyed braless teenager in a *Life, Live It* t-shirt, and a petite young mother in pink with a cherubic little boy in short pants and a Mickey Mouse hat. Unless the enigmatic Mr. Beaumarchaise was also a master of disguise, he was not among us.

As our Societe Nationale des Chermin de Fer five-car special picked up speed on the straightaway, I knew I had less than ten minutes to check the remaining cars before we pulled into Pornichet. I gave quick consideration to the lifelong damage to my lungs that a walk through the vacuum packed rolling smoke houses would cause, and decided the health of an amateur historian was secondary to his passion to encounter a national treasure, a man-god who, by the mere mention of his name evoked the magic to erase any memory of the rain-drenched, moody blue-gray day around us.

I exited the bathroom with several wads of water-soaked toilet paper held to my nose and mouth and walked right into a startled conductor, who gave every indication he thought I was getting ready to pull the first train heist in French rail history. My faulty command of his language did not include, "This is only a make-shift anti-nicotine mask," so I cut to the chase, "Do you happen to know if Monsieur Beaumarchaise is on the train yet?"

When monsieur Cherubic Short Pants ran up to him and asked the same question, about four octaves higher than me. The conductor relaxed his jaw line long enough to birth a genuine smile and say," I haven't seen him, but you never know with that fellow. No, no, not yet. I'm sure." He backed away still focusing on my dripping wads, and quickly disappeared into another car. I seized the moment, went to one knee and asked Short Pants, "Who is this chap, Beaumarchaise?" He didn't have a chance to move his lips before Madam Pink Lady grabbed his arm and yanked him halfway across the car, landing in his seat with a thud. From the ominous stares of the non-smokers it was obvious I had gone from train robber to potential child molester in less than sixty seconds.

It was time for quiet reflection.

I turned to my rain-sprayed window to the French countryside and watched the last views of the port of La Baul with the large blue sign announcing, "La Plus Plage in Europe", *the best beach in Europe.* More fact than boast. Three miles of a perfect half-moon bay enclosing clear, sparkling Mediterranean blue water. A fleet of finely polished white yachts and expensive power boats filled the marinas in stark contrast to the fifteenth century flower-covered stone cottages nearby. Famous named European boutiques rushed by, so did grand hotels, smart restaurants, the neon glitz of a new casino followed by the traditional charm of flamboyant Gothic and Renaissance designed streets reluctantly surrendering under an all-out assault from fast food joints, cola dispensers, and souvenir shops. Suddenly, the large rivulets of rain water crisscrossing my window seemed more like tear drops from a proud ancient land fading into its own history.

Soon the hum of high-speed wheel on track was lulling us all into quiet pursuits. Mrs. Ben Franklin was deep inside Balzac's *La Comedie Humaine,* the backpackers were asleep, Madam Pink was methodically moving from clue to answer in her Match Magazine crossword, while

Short Pants stroked his crayons in the Monsieur Goofy Coloring Book with the definite intensity of Gauguin before a nude.

Outside picture-perfect postcards of time-warped marshlands, salt-pans, canalized waterways probing deep into enchanting medieval towns, fishing villages, and bridges over flower-filled moats. Seventeenth and eighteenth century France was alive again. It stopped raining. My window was clear.

Strange how peaceful and motionless nature can make you feel at eighty-five miles an hour.

That would soon end.

"Pornichet, Pornichet", the conductor announced as we slowed down into our first stop, an old wooden railway depot pockmarked with sixty-year-old bullet holes, proud remnants of the intense fighting in WW II to liberate the small hamlet. A minor commotion at the far end of the platform drew everybody's attention. An old man with a very large head under a red beret was holding court before some enthusiastic disciples. He waved his hands and spoke in loud measured tones like a conquering Roman before his victorious legions. They cheered. He patted them on the shoulders. They cheered. He started singing. They cheered. His female companion, a large woman with immense hands and a menacing scowl was ignoring the adulation and pushing him up on to the train. She pushed; he resisted. She pushed harder; he sang louder. Always, they cheered. He resisted. She won. They were now both on board.

You could feel the sudden burst of vitality transforming the peaceful monotony of the 557 from La Baul to Paris like an outrageously colorful boutonniere being placed on an old jacket. From the sounds of laughter and cheers rolling from one car to another, it was certain that everyone's favorite uncle had come to call. It had to be the great man himself. Let the revels begin. Beaumarchaise has arrived. The door to our car swung open, and the smiling conductor bowed and pointed to the two seats next to me. The Large Woman, muttering inaudibly to herself, took the one farthest from me. Suddenly the room filled with the sweet smell of lime musk cologne as the greatest boulevardier of them all, a red-faced beaming Maurice Chevalier look-a-like filled the entire doorway. With several ribbons streaming down from his beret around his broad shoulders, he was impeccably dressed in a shiny black tuxedo with nine, count them, nine rows of medals and multicolored combat decorations across his Bunyanesque chest. The unmistakable green ribbon ribbed with seven red stripes holding the crossed swords medallion of the Croix de Guerre hung around his thick, bulging neck. If ever Zeus took living form and rode a train, it was now.

"Bonjour mes amis, bonjour," he graciously bellowed as we all answered a silent command and immediately sat at attention in unison.

A startled Mrs. Franklin dropped her Balzac. The Great One bent down, retrieved it, and kissed her hand before carefully placing the book back in her clutches. He bellowed again, shook everybody's hand, laughed, hummed a few bars of a cheery little ditty that could easily have passed as a Frencified *Roll Out The Barrel* and then exclaimed, "Today is a great day. Tomorrow will be even better." There could be no resistance to this infectious vitality. We all applauded. I couldn't imagine Professor Harold Hill and all his seventy-six trombones making a more spirited entrance.

Here was a sunshine warrior of the first magnitude, and he could not be denied. He clapped his hands the way giants do when they're happy, tipped his beret, and sat down—next to me. For once the gods were on my side. I could smell through the muted lime to a hint of summer jasmine. He was probably well past eighty but his smiling life force and bubbling candor made him younger than all of us. He extended his bear claw of a hand, "Comment allez-vous? Mon nom...", I stopped him in mid sentence. "I know who you are, sir, and it's an honor to meet you." The Large Lady made a muffled sound of distain and turned away. Those would be my last words to the great man. Like all myths, he was above earthbound conversation. He would recognize you with a knowing smile, but had no need to listen and respond to mere mortals. He had seen things and climbed mountains others could never understand, so he cheerfully fed off his own memory and spoke in one long run-on sentence after another about things that interested him. His encyclopedic recall was spellbinding.

"Don't be fooled, my friend, nothing is what it appears on the train from La Baul to Paris. It started in 1917, and continued through '45—spies, double agents, foreign correspondents in search of intrigue, traitors in exile, small men dressed in tweed carrying top secret documents to the front, suicidal young poets, forbidden lovers on a dangerous tryst, each pretending to be the contented bourgeois traveler—not so."

He hammered his cannonball fist on the arm rest and drew more inaudible mumbling from the Large Woman, now engaged in threading two long silver knitting needles. Undisturbed, he continued, "...the fates of nations, perhaps the world, was decided on this run. True. Do you know that Jacques LeBecque himself once sat in your seat? Can you believe who was sitting opposite him? None other than Heinrich Volstad. Imagine, the head of the Gestapo in occupied western France making small talk with the leader of the French Resistance, each unaware he was discussing the weather with his mortal enemy. Ah, now there is a part of the soap opera of history you will not read in books."

He crossed his arms on his lap and was momentarily lost in another time, but not enough to miss the fact we were speeding past another old train station.

"Ah, Bats Sur Mere. Are you aware Madame, your friend Balzac wrote his novel *Beatrix* along the cliffs above the beach right here?" He didn't wait for her response, and she gave none.

He continued his disjointed soliloquy for another hour.

He quoted Whitman, Tennyson, Churchill, Omar Khayyam, and Richard III. I learned that Bluebeard, the pirate, had been a great soldier who rode with Joan of Arc and had become a Marshall of France before losing his head in that large castle off in the distant mist. He pointed to the exact spot in the coastal road above St. Nazaire where Pershing's American Expeditionary Force landed in 1918. He appeared near tears as he saluted the obelisk in the harbor commemorating the fallen heroes of "Operation Chariot."

"It was the greatest daring raid of all time, my friends," he said in subdued, dramatic tones, "carried out by 265 brave British commandos in 1942. Only 50 survived." Again, he snapped a smart salute. But the Great Man wasn't one to sustain a mood any longer than it took to reach his next thought, and that could be a flawless recitation of the preamble to the Napoleonic Codes, or a detailed description of Rochambeau's tactics leading the French army against the English in the American Revolutionary War, or where to find the best macaroons on the Left Bank.

The fact that everyone else had lost interest in being in close proximity to a national icon and had resumed their sedentary preoccupations had no effect on his never-ending presentation.

On and on he went. I alone remained riveted to each new narrative waiting for the moment he revealed the reason he was one of France's most honored sons. It never came, but no matter.

Perhaps, I needed the benediction of someone or something greater than myself to validate my journey. Perhaps that, or maybe the seduction of mere fascination with a colorful hero who seems to have experienced achievement at that dangerous but magical level of survival the rest of us can only imagine.

As we sped toward Nantes, the capital city of Brittany, I had mastered the art of divided attention. One ear to the master and both eyes on the flat, lush countryside rolling by. Perfect carpets of green surrounding symmetrical parcels of farmland, granite churches, sprawling castles with ramparts still intact, housing the story of empires long departed, alongside soccer fields, thatch-roofed cottages and gingerbread villages where time was a lazy afterthought.

At Nantes, the train swelled to standing-room only capacity. The Great One "Bonjoured" and shook hands with every one of the 17 new passengers restocking our non-smoking kiosk and continued his rambling elocution.

A sudden violent downpour emptied the station of all movement, except one fearless little chap strutting the water-soaked platform with great pride and regal unconcern, like Wellington defying the French canon at Waterloo. His glistening black velvet body was interrupted by a bright white spot covering his rounded chest. His beak was red and the comb sweeping back from his crown was sunset orange.

If birds have personalities then Mr. Black and White was surely the maitre'd at the supremely superior Hotel Deauville or perhaps the Governor-General of a distant colony. Cocky, confident, the king's musketeer. Relentlessly self-regarding in every staccato movement. While rain, wind and three loud blasts of the train whistle would send every other of his skittish species to flight, Mr.Black and White wasn't phased a bit. Could he be the ornithological missing link or was he just eminently French?

My militant divided attention was gone. This remarkable tiny field marshall had it all. He jumped down to the tracks opposite my window and began a full-scale inspection of the train's undercarriage from stem to stern, like a diva inspecting the chorus before the curtain goes up.

Suddenly, the entire train tilted slightly to the left. It woke one of the backpackers who asked the conductor, "What's the matter?"

"Monsieur Beaumarchaise has arrived," he shouted with a giddy lilt to his voice.

Short Pants was uncontrollable, cheering at the top of his lungs, "Monsieur Beaumarchais! Monsieur Beaumarchais!"

Now everyone in our car rushed to the windows and began laughing and cheering like children at the final school bell. Flash bulbs popped. Even the Great One stopped his marathon monologue and was unceremoniously pushing me out of my seat to get to the window.

I tugged at the conductor's coat, "What are you talking about? *This* is Mr. Beaumarchaise," pointing to the hovering Great One.

"No, monsieur, *that* is Mr. Beaumarchaise," pointing down at the track.

"The bird?"

"Not any bird, monsieur. France's most famous commuter. Mr.Beaumarchaise boards our train every day and travels with us to Paris and back. Watch."

Just as the 557 started to roll forward, the former Mr. Black and White flies to the top of the platform as if making a last minute check of his accommodations and then flies to the top our locomotive where he sits majestically on the engineer's canopy. The king is on his throne. Long live the king! The cars are rocked with a new, more animated cheering followed by a high-pitched chatter known to every Olympic champion when he enters a room filled with admirers. Perhaps the French are not so blasé after all.

The former Great One continued to talk for the final one hour run to Paris. I didn't hear a word he said.

As The Large Women brushed past me on her way to the exit, her mumbling became audible, "He's just an old fool who buys his medals in stores."

As I exited, France's most famous feathered bon vivant flew off the top of the baggage car into the rafters of Montparnasse to a larger chorus of cheers and applause.

Forty-five minutes later, as the 557 became the 558 and started to retrace its run back from whence it came, the largest train depot in France was once again rocked with applause. The legend of Monsieur Beaumarchaise was growing. He was back at his command post above it all heading home.

Now, I was mumbling, "Nothing is what it appears on the train from La Baul to Paris."

WHITE MAN'S RAGE

Joe called today.

"So whydahell haven't you called?! I'm tired of pursuing the people I love, pal. Pick up the damn phone and call once in awhile. Hello, how are ya'? Howyadoin? Are you dying of cancer or what? Communicate, you know, talk, words, phrases, the kind of stuff that comes out when you open your mouth. I mean, let's face it, just like that character in Eugene O'Neill's one-act play, you know, where that Broadway down-and-outer chewed the ear off that poor slob in that flea bag. What was it?"

"Hughie."

"Hughie, yeah, right. We're the only ones we can really talk to. Know what I mean?"

"I know."

"Of course, you know. Hell, we're the only ones left on this miserable planet who still play Harry James and Guy Lombardo. (Singing) *Boo-hoo, you left me crying for you…*Jesus H. Christ, what ever happened to lyrics, words you understood, music that didn't want to make you pick an Uzi and blast the living shit outta your mailman? Oh, excuse me, mail person. Christ, what's happened to words? I don't recognize them anymore. Would somebody please tell me whatdahell is so gay about being a fag? Can you believe this, my boxman down at the plant wanted to take off a few days because it was Gay Pride Week, for crissakes? When I said, 'no way,' the little shit filed a *sexual harassment* complaint against me. Said I had *homophobia*, for crissakes. That I wasn't gender neutral...I didn't respect alternate lifestyles. Call me old fashioned, but one guy sticking his joystick up another guy's poop chute is no goddamn alternative in my book, period. Where do these words come from? Significant other, drug *dependent*—oh there's a beauty. What is it, you wake up one morning, you catch a bug like the flu and you got symptoms, right? Outta your control, right? What is it? A runny nose, diarrhea, little chest congestion followed by this irresistible urge to shove a ton and a half of cocaine up your ass or wherever-dahell they shove it. (Sarcastic) Oh, sure, you can't help it. You've got this *dependency.* Now we're equating drug addiction with being a choc-oholic, for crissakes. There's no right and wrong anymore. Everything is tolerated. Politicians don't lie, they just *mis-speak.* And I'd better not get sick because my medical co-payments are higher than the goddamn national debt of Brazil. But a fuckin' illegal alien crosses the border in a tunnel and, hey, come on over, free medical care, bring your kids, too, and we'll throw in a free education. And they don't even have to speak English, God forbid, we should *discriminate* in our brave new *multi-culture* society. And how about those millionaire primadonnas in the major leagues—knocking up fifteen-year-old girls, in and out of drug and alcohol rehab? Hey, no problem. It's cool to be *bad, Man.* Screw up as many times as you want. Three, four, five times. Your cen-terfielder's job is waiting for you. Hell, we'll even throw in an extra two million on your next contract. You can write a book. Cry with Oprah. It's not your fault. It's just that sensitive *inner child* of yours rebelling against your evil *dysfuctional* family. Shit, shit, shit! Nobody's responsi-ble anymore. The two Neanderthal punks who kicked and beat that truck driver with forty million people watching the riots on TV a few years back—ahh, I did it again, forgive my *political incorrectness*, it wasn't a riot, it was a *rebellion*, a social statement. Hey, they weren't responsible. Not their fault. All that looting, burning and head bashing was just an uncontrollable *inner rage* that had to express itself, for crissakes. I'm going to the window, Charley. I'm opening the window right now (shouting), and I'm going to express *my* inner goddamn rage.

'No more car alarms at two in the morning or so help me I'll stick a flamethrower up your fuckin' exhaust pipe. And turn off that goddamn rap music. Music? Christ! I've heard large animals passing wind that sounded more rhythmic than that shit. Nothing but Tommy Dorsey and Lawrence Welk until further notice. THAT'S AN ORDER!'"

(Calmed down) What's going on here, Charley. Something's wrong when the last good thing I can remember is Jackie Robinson stealing home against the Giants."

"Thursday, September 3, 1949, two-forty-three in the afternoon. Ebbets Field."

"Right. I remember looking at the scoreboard clock above the Abe Stark Clothing sign. You know, I had a feeling it would be the last beautiful thing I would ever see. I dunno. I get up in the morning, wash my teeth, put on my socks, and go to work. I put in my time but I'm not really here, you know what I mean?"

"I know what you mean, Joe."

"I recognize my own voice so I know it's me but that's it. I don't recognize anything else going on. I know, I know, I can hear you saying, 'You gotta' go with the flow, Joe. Go with the flow.' Howdahell can I go with the flow when the flow is wearing it's hat on backwards, dark sunglasses at night, for crissakes, and a pair of baggy pants that would be two sizes too big for King Kong, for crissakes. I don't know what America means anymore. I can't find my history anywhere. Know what I mean? Maybe I'm just lonely. Who am I kidding? Of course, I'm lonely. I was born to be married. Did a damn good job of it for twenty-six years, let's face it, and then, poof! The kids are gone, she's gone, and I'm giving up half my paycheck so she can sip Margaritas and screw some beachboy in Cabo San Lucas, for crissakes. Okay,

okay, water under the bridge, you say. Ehhh, did I tell you I'm flying up to Bridgeport this weekend?"

"No, you didn't."

"You know, I've been seeing this lady up there for a year now and, well, she wants to get married and I think maybe I want to, but, hell, well, she's a real strict Catholic and has this thing about no sex before marriage. I know, I know—sounds a little loop-de-loo for this day and age, but, hell, she's like us. She's from another time, you know. I'm frustrated as hell, but I respect that. Hell, if this was 1955 I wouldn't think twice about marrying her, but it's 1995, and, God, I never thought I'd be saying this—I don't think I can commit to one woman for the rest of my life. I don't know why I can't, but I just can't. I keep telling myself it's because, hey, what happens after we get married, have sex, and it doesn't work. What? I get divorced again, she gets the other half of my paycheck, and I'm clipping coupons and living at the Y. Nah, that's not it. Who am I kidding? Whatdahell went wrong, Charley? And where is the Lone Ranger when you need him? I'm fifty-nine-years old, afraid to die alone, and afraid to do anything about it. Christ, I hate being a cripple before I'm a cripple. Know what I mean? So, I'll go to Bridgeport. We'll hold hands. She'll read me some gooey crap from *The Bridges of Madison County.* We'll do some Catholic kissing, and I'll pretend I'm not the horniest senior citizen on the East Coast. We'll each say we need a little more time, and ba-da-bing-ba-da-boom, etcetera, etcetera. Tell me, Charley, now can you tell me howdahell can you make a decision when you don't know where you are anymore? Can you tell me that?

"Well, I think…"

(He laughed halfheartedly) Funny, ain't it, Charley. Guys like you and I always knew what the score was. We just never figured they'd come along and change the game. Well, I'd better be going. Eh, did I tell ya I'll be going in Thursday for triple by-pass surgery? Hey, no big thing, not nowadays. They blow out a few pipes. Wham bam, thank you ma'am. You're home in three days. It's all routine. I'm not worried a bit. Eh, listen, Charley, no need to come up and see me. You know how I hate visitors when I'm in the tank—candy, balloons, small talk. No way. I'm fine. Not worried a bit. I'll just watch a little TV, play some Tommy Dorsey. I'll be fine. Boy, thank God we've still got the old music, eh. (Sings) *Missed the Saturday dance...heard they crowded the floor. Couldn't bear it without you...don't get around much anymore..."*

"I'll come up to see you."

"Didn't I tell you I don't want you to do that? You know your problem, Charley?"

"I never listen, right?"

"Right. I'll call you when I get out. Goodbye, Boobie."

JOE CALLED BACK

Joe called today.

"So, boobie, I've been waiting."

"Waiting for what?"

"Your call. You said last time you'd call me back. That was two weeks ago."

"No, Joe, you were supposed to call me, remember?"

"No. Ah, whatdahell difference does it make? That bastard O. J. Simpson gets away with murder; the Jews kill their own Prime Minister; and that fuckin' heartless traitor, Art Modell, is moving the Cleveland Browns to fuckin' Baltimore because the Colts moved to Indianapolis, for crissakes; and the New York Giants are still called the New York Giants even though they're playing all their games in goddamn *New Jersey;* and some poor schmuck found a goddamn frog in his burrito at El Torida, for crissakes, and we're arguin 'over who's supposed to call who. Whatdafuck is going on?"

"So, how are you, Joe? Did you marry that lady from Bridgeport?"

"I don't know what I'm doin'. No, I didn't. You know why? Because I can't picture myself sitting in my underwear reading the morning paper in her company. Is that a kick in the ass or what? A sixty-year old millionairess with the body of a Playboy centerfold—

yeah, no kiddin', loves me madly, wants to spend the rest of her life with me and I can't do it because she's just not the kind of gal you walk around in your under-wear in front of. And, you know me, I like to walk around in my skivvies, goddamnit. Listen to this. She wants to get married in goddamn Hawaii beside a waterfall with Don Ho singing 'Somewhere Beyond The Reef,' for crissakes. She says don't worry about money. We can live in her seven-bedroom house. Like hell! Doilies! She's got doilies, for crissakes, on the back of all the chairs. I can't live in a house with doilies. And whydahell are these things important, you say? I don't know, but they are. I guess maybe when you get our age, you get used to a lot of little things that don't add up to a hell-evalot to anybody else but to you. Well, they're your life. Know what I mean? And you don't want to hide them just because you're married to Mary Poppins. Whatdahell does all this come down to Charley?"

"I dunno. Maybe you want companionship, but you're not willing to put up with doilies to get it, maybe."

"I'm serious here, Charley. I'm fifty-nine years old. I don't recognize a damn thing on television, and I'm right back where I started from—living in a one-bedroom house that's falling down around me, and I can't fix it because I don't have a pot to piss in. Nothing means anything to me anymore. I'm mad at everybody. I'm giving the finger to people on the freeway now—little old ladies, cops, school bus drivers. I don't give a damn. I'm an equal opportunity bird flipper.

And I can't stand what's happening to this country, and I don't know who to blame. Am I going nuts, Charley?"

"Everybody over fifty is nuts, Joe."

"Jeez, I hate getting old, Charley. I hate not having a dream anymore. Know what I mean? Hey, pal of mine, howcum you didn't ask me about my heart surgery? I could have croaked on the operating table for all you care."

"Joe, Joe, I held your hand for seven hours in the recovery room. Don't you remember? We sang the entire score from South Pacific."

"Was that you? Christ, I thought I was dreaming. All that goddamn anesthetic they pump you up with. They go overboard, I swear."

(Playfully sarcastic) "Right, next time they cut a two-foot hole in your chest, hook your heart up to a pump, chop away five diseased arteries, and replace all your cardiac valves, just ask for a little Tylenol instead. That way, at least, you'll be sure to remember the post operative sing-a-long."

(Both singing) *"We got moonlight on the sea…we got mangoes and bananas you can pick right off the tree…we got volleyball and ping pong and a lot of dandy games…what ain't we got? We ain't got dames!"*

Joe continues.

"What's happened, Charley? Why do I keep calling you with the same conversation all the time?"

"I dunno. Maybe we just want to be young again. Maybe we just don't like the sound of chapters closing, maybe."

"You think that's it? I think it's all those goddamn phony peace-and-love hippies from the sixties who went around screwing one another every hour, and now their brain-dead, drug-drenched, ghetto-blasting, rap-music-loving airhead kids are running the country. Flower children, my ass. Unemployed losers. Whydahell did we allow society's garbage to take over the farm, Charley? Why? They were against everything, the war, government, education, morality, people over forty, everything. But what were they *for*, Charley? They never told us what they were for. You know why? Because they weren't for anything. Burn, baby, burn down the establishment, but they never told us what they were going to build in its place. That's why we're screwed up today, Charley. Everybody's tearing things down; nobody's building. Christ, we should have bombed UC Berkeley instead of Hanoi. And don't get me started over that damn fucked up, Jane Fonda."

Charley starts singing over Joe's tirade.

"Happy talkie talk, keep talking happy talk. Talk about things you like to do…"

"What a fourteen-carat phony bitch. Anti-war hero, my ass."

"You got to have a dream, if you don't have a dream, how you gonna have a dream come true. Talk about a boy...."

Joe starts singing.

"...saying to der girl..."

Charley, alone.

"You and I are lucky to be us...hit it, Joe."

Together.

"Happy talkie talk. Keep talking happy talk. Talk about things you love to do. You gotta have a dream. If you don't have a dream...how you gonna have a dream come true...la la la la la la...hmnnn, hmnnn"

Pause. Joe speaks.

"I've lost a lot of good stuff in my life, but as long as I got you, pal, on the other end of a phone, I'm going to be fine."

"Ditto, Joe. Ditto."

"Stay in touch. I'll see ya'"

JOE HASN'T CALLED
IN AWHILE

Hadn't heard from Joe in a year, so I called.

"Hey, Joey, baby, sweetheart, howyadoin', pal?

"Never mind that crap. So homcum you never call?"

"I'm calling right now, ain't I? Besides, what's wrong with your dialing finger?"

"My dialing finger is fine. I wish I could say the same for my prostate, but, hey, time marches on. So, howcum I didn't get a congratulations card or a flower or a late model Italian sports car from my occasional best friend?"

"Whadahell are you talking about? Did you win the lottery or what?"

"I got married, for crissakes. Oops, sorry honey. She's in the next room. Doesn't like me cursing. Promised her I'd cut down."

"Married, married. Hey, Joe, congratulations. You did it. Who's the lucky miss?"

"You remember, the gal from Bridgeport, the no sex before marriage Catholic I was telling you about? Yeah, hell, I woke up one day and said, 'Look, Joe, what are your options? Eat cold cereal three times a day, feel sorry for yourself, and watch the liver spots on the back of your hands grow, or get the decent companionship you need?' Let's face it, Charley, some guys just have to be married, whether they like it or not. Hey, I'm not saying I don't like it. Hell, she's a wonderful person. And we get along. That's important, Charley, comfortability. When you're young and lugging around a hard-on all day, you never think about comfortability, but the day after you blow out sixty-one candles on your freakin' birth-day cake, it becomes important. Jeez, makes you stop and think just how much of your life is determined by your cock. Que sera, sera. Men are from Mars, women are from Vegas."

"Venus, Joe. Women are from Venus."

"Yeah, whatever. It's all crap. I read it. Three hundred pages of 'how to read the other person's signs,' for crissakes. Shit like when she says, 'Don't touch me,' she really means 'Touch me.' 'I need to be alone' means 'I don't want to be alone.' I can't believe it, Charley. We've been on this earth, what, forty million years, and women still don't know men just want to get laid. Period. Everything else is penance, for crissakes. Men are wild horses, we don't want a nest, we want a campsite. We just want to pick up and gallop off anytime we please. Enough with these phony books and seminars. It's nature, for crissakes. Men can't help it. Women think just because they put a saddle on us, we're housebroken. We're not. Didya ever get close to an Alaskan timber wolf, Charley?"

"No, I try to keep my distance. Why?"

"They're always looking to the wilderness, like someone or something is always calling them to leave whatever they're doing and run off to follow their nature. They always know wherever they are is not where they're supposed to be. It's the same with men."

"Wild horses and timber wolves, eh?"

"That's us. I was watching a documentary the other night on the A&E Channel—that's the only thing I'm watching these days—that and the Black Entertainment Network."

"Black Entertainment Network? Eh, Joe, your new wife, is she, eh..."

"No, no. She's as white as a snowflake. She just wants me to open up my thinking, you know, understand this new can't-we-just-get-along-with-black thing. It's an interesting channel. Did you know that Hannibal was black?"

"No, I knew he was a dwarf, but..."

"Christ, he was black and a dwarf? They never said anything about that. Talk about double jeopardy. Did you know Hitler was a her-maphrodite, you know, had an ingrown penis?"

"What was Hitler doing on the Black Entertainment Network? Don't tell me he was a brother, too?"

"No, I'm talking about A&E. There's a great six-part series on the psychology of The Fuhrer. There's a theory because his organ wasn't outside, you know, he had this great inferiority complex and so he had to grab all that power."

"What are you saying? If Hitler were hung a little better, we could have avoided World War II?"

We both laugh.

"So, Joe, come on. Tell me about married life. Happy? Where you living? You still eating cold cereal? Sex, how is it? Come on, give."

"You know, Charley, Bettina, that's my new wife, has made me real-ize my first wife was just a girl, and she's a lady. There's a big differ-ence."

"Like what?"

"She's just...understanding, you know. I need my space; she under-stands. I need to rant and rave about this and that, and she smiles and walks away. Let's me do my thing. No whining. No moaning. No guilt trips. She understands. She's mature. She's a lady. Oh sure, you never get everything. Life's always a tradeoff."

You're lonely, you get married. You're not lonely anymore, but you gotta stop being selfish, you know, and learn to compromise, do what she wants to do sometimes, even though you can't stand doing it.

Now, I'm not saying I can't stand it, mind you, just, you know, you need time to adjust. Like my having to convert to Catholicism, after being a non-religious Jew, for sixty years, or she wouldn't go through with it. Stuff like that. Your mind says you're married, but your body says you're still a bachelor."

"What are you saying, Joe?"

"I'm saying I don't particularly want to go back to fuckin' Bridgeport, Connecticut, in the middle of fuckin' January, for crissakes, but I'm goin.'"

"Hey, hey Joe. Watch your language. Your wife, remember?"

"It's alright, I moved into the closet. I told you, Bettina has this big house back there, and wants to spend six months there and six months here in L.A. I mean, Christ, that's why I moved from the East Coast twenty years ago—to get away from all that snow, the relatives, the whole thing. But, whatdahell, you pay the price, you know. You're married."

"So, how's the sex, pal?"

"Well, you know, it's…married sex."

"Whatdahell does that mean?"

"Come on, you were married once. You know."

"You mean your new bride falls asleep in the middle of a hump?"

"I mean it's…comfortable. Hell, at this age you can't expect rockets red glare, bombs bursting in air, boom da boom, da boom. It's a different kind of satisfaction, you know. Hell, Charley, I'm happy. I've got a partner, a very good woman to share things with. Okay, she's having a hard time adjusting to my ways." "You walking around in your underwear again?"

"Only in the kitchen and the basement."

"You compromised, right?"

"Right. That's the least I can do for all the companionship she's giving me.

She doesn't want me staying up late watching TV, fine. No problem, I'll go to bed at goddamn nine o'clock, if it makes her happy. These are small things."

Pause.

"Well, Joe, my friend, I'm happy for you. Man was not meant to be alone, except on bowling nights. And you sound like you've got a good lady—and that's a lot."

"Yeah, it is. So how about I call you in a week or so?"

"Great. Well, take care, pal. Maybe we can get together, and, who knows, watch a couple of timber wolves or something."

THE LAST TIME I EVER HEARD FROM JOE

"Hello, boobie, it's me, Joe. So, howareya? I know, I know, you haven't heard from me in a year, and you're thinking 'Whatdahell is with this guy? He gets married, forgets his friends, because he doesn't need them anymore, got it made, old lady's got plenty of dough, has nothing to worry about.' Yeah, yeah, I hear ya' but it's not true. It's just, well, things change when you're married. You know. I don't mean you forget your friends. You just, well, live in a smaller circle. You have to focus more on the other person. Not that she needs my constant approval or anything like that. Hell, no, this is a very independent president of the East Bridgeport Junior League. No sweet, fragile little porcelain doll, here. No sir. She could do very nicely on her own, thank you. So, how are ya'?"

"Thanks for asking. I have leprosy attacking every major organ, there a raging fire in my living room right now, and I'm thinking of strapping on a hundred pounds of dynamite and walking into work later on."

Joe isn't listening.

"Good, good. So, how's the weather down there?"

"Joe, Joe, time out. Listen to me. Why did you call? What's going on?"

"What, something has to be going on to call a friend?"

"Cut the bullshit. I've known you since you borrowed my Waterman's fountain pen in first grade, and never returned it. This is your 'I'm wrestling with a big time problem' voice. So cut to the chase. The marriage isn't working? You can't get it up, anymore? What?"

Pause.

"I've got this opportunity to, eh,—it's hard to say it."

"Who is she?"

"Some gal I knew way back when. It's crazy, I know. I love my wife. She's a wonderful person, really. We do everything together. She knows when to give me my space, when to buck me up. This woman is the companion every man wants to grow old with, I'm telling you. And she'll do anything for me in bed, you know. Whydahell am I even thinking about doing this?"

"Hey, every married man thinks about it all the time. It's just that happily married men feel guilty about it, that's all."

"Charley, that's it. I don't feel guilty. I want to feel guilty, but hell, I don't know what I feel. But this other woman is pure lust, you know. She makes everything inside of me work right away. I don't have to think about pretending to be involved or worrying whether or not I'm gonna be able to get the horse out of the barn or not. I just know it's gonna be the greatest sex I'll ever have, and, hey, I'm sixty-one. This is my last shot."

"You're married. You got a shot every night."

"Now, who's not listening? It's not the same, Charley. Not the same."

"So who is this incredible lay? Do I know her?"

"No, no. I met her when I was in the service. She worked in the Army PX. I went in one day to buy a can of Prince Albert, and I couldn't keep my eyes off her. I swear she was an angel in a navy blue dress. We talked and laughed for hours. I met her after work. We just looked at one another, and it just kind of happened by itself. We went to a motel. It wasn't dirty. It was sweet. We were so naïve. I remember We both registered under our own names. Can you believe that? It was the last time I felt real magic in my life. We held one another all night and the next morning. There hasn't been a day gone by that I haven't thought about that beautiful young girl in a navy blue dress. I think sometimes she was the only thing that kept me going."

"Well, it's all part of the allotment. You get some body parts, a brain, a little time, a social security card, and one night of incredible lust to remember the rest of your life. We've all had it, Joe, but it never becomes part of the routine. It's not in the master plan. It's just a one shot-promotion thrown in to hold your interest, pal."

"Yeah, but she's back. Last Tuesday I got this letter from her. Said she's been looking for me for thirty years. Said she needs to be with me like it was before. Enclosed a photo. What a body. Nothing's changed. She's drop-dead gorgeous. I'd send you an email picture, but I never learned how to use that damn attachment function. Wants to meet me at her hotel room in the Valley tonight. And it would be easy. My wife is in Canada visiting her son for a few days. I don't understand why a man with a great wife would want to risk losing it all for just one more night in the Magic Kingdom."

"It's one of the enduring mysteries of our planet, right up there with gravity and Martha Stewart. So, are you going to do it?"

"God, I hope not, but I think I am. Funny, you think you control things like this. You know the right thing to do is to stay faithful, but some things are bigger than reason. You know what I mean? You think women feel this way?"

"Hell, yes. Your old lady is probably boffing a Royal Canadian Mountie as we speak."

We laugh, but Joe's laugh is more like a faint smile with a barely audible "yeah."

"Well, I got to go separate the garbage."

"What?"

"They pick up early in the morning. My wife is a stickler, you know, paper in the green barrel, glass and all the other crap in the black barrel. Drives me nuts, but whadahell."

"Let me get this straight. First you separate the garbage and then you go cheat on your wife in the valley?"

"You make it sound so—tawdry."

"How about self-destructive, is that better?"

"Come on, I need this thing. I don't know why, but I do."

"Joe, you need excitement. You don't need adultery in Van Nuys. Put on a Count Basie 78. Try 'Two O'Clock Jump.' Dance around the room in a funny hat, something. Believe me, it'll pass."

"You don't understand."

"I understand we're looking in the mirror every day, and we don't like the old guy looking back at us. We want to keep that seventeen-year-old boy inside alive, and we don't know how. Face it, Joe, we're afraid of dying, and a romp in the hay is a way of fooling ourselves for a few minutes it ain't gonna happen. But it is. We're gonna die, pal. The sooner we face it and move on with the rest of our lives, the better things get."

Pause.

"Funny, Charley."

"What?"

"I've been thinking a lot about dying lately. I mean I'm not morbid or anything. It just hits me all of a sudden at the strangest times, you know, shaving, walking in the park, looking at a young kid playing with his father. Then I hear this little voice saying if I don't do this, I'll wonder the rest of my life what I missed."

"Yeah, and if you do it, then you'll have nothing to wonder about the rest of your life. That's pretty dull."

"Boy, I'm really confused."

"Hey, go put the garbage out, then say five Hail Mary's, six Our Father's, and make a good Act of Contrition."

They laugh. Joe's isn't as weak as before.

"You know something, Charley?"

"What's that, pal?"

"You're a damn good friend. We ought to spend more time together. Maybe you'll come over for some meatloaf some night soon, huh?"

"Sounds good. Just let me know."

"I'll see ya', Charley, and thanks. Thanks a lot."

"Goodbye, Joe."

That was the last time I ever spoke to Joe. A few hours later, paramedics were summoned to a hotel room in the Valley. It was too late. His companion at the time, a very pretty lady in a navy blue dress was inconsolable, "I don't understand. We just sat around talking and laughing. He was having such a good time...then he just closed his eyes and..."

A PIECE OF FILM

"You've got to have a piece of film on yourself, or you'll never have a shot in this town." It's a sentence wielded by casting directors and agents like a flaming ax incessantly pounding the soul of every struggling actor in Hollywood. You just can't be considered for an audition until you can verify someone else has taken a chance on you and emulsified your image on film. Simply, you've got to have been in someone else's film before you can get a job in somebody else's film.

So if you're in the vast majority of actors who have exited the birth canal sans a can of 35 mm film on previous performances, you face this daunting conundrum every waking moment of your artistic life.

Dave Engelman never thought about this challenge for the first forty-eight years of his existence. He was too busy working two jobs to afford his alimony and support two children the court was disposed to award him. Now they were grown and out the door.

Time to pursue the dream.

Dave wanted to grab a small piece of celluloid immortality, create magic, be bigger than the sum total of his humdrum existence in Peoria, Illinois. He wanted to be a Hollywood actor.

The fact that he had never stepped onto a stage or read a piece of dialogue in front of anyone or anything other than his bathroom mirror didn't dull his theatrical passion a bit. And he didn't fool himself either, when he looked into that mirror. He saw what the world saw. A gawky, gangly six-foot eight, middle-aged man with sunken cheeks, and the sallow complexion of an ill-fed penitent monk battling rheumatoid arthritis in every joint of his body.

He came from two hundred years of sensible Midwest farm stock. He was a practical man. He knew unless Hollywood was looking to redo the life story of Icabod Crane, he had more of a chance to tango on the moon than land a part in the movies. But dreamers rarely consider the odds, so he packed up some modest belongings in his rusting '64 Ford Fairlane and headed west.

I met Dave in the summer of '74, when I joined a small band of actors performing in a thinly disguised pickle factory in the shadow of the famed Hollywood sign. We did several plays and could have made more of a dent in the collective consciousness of industry talent scouts, if we were all enrolled in the Federal Witness Protection Program. Dave held spears in the crowd scenes and was, by far, the best volunteer prop man in the fickle life of the little theater movement in Los Angeles, but he never got a chance to speak a single line of dialogue in any play.

And things got no better in the next seven years—more little theater plays; more anonymity in a crowd, more rehearsing auditioning scenes that no one wanted to see.

Actors are a superstitious lot. They'll never label a fellow performer a "bad actor," no matter how untalented the chap may be, for fear the gods of the muse will jinx their own quest for acceptance. But the undeniable fact—even to those of us who admired and respected his dogged determination and infinite hope that somewhere, sometime, his face would flicker across the screen of a darkened theater, was that there was a reason he had never won a speaking role on stage or secured a paid day's work in a film.

Dave Engleman, for all his super-charged belief in the American myth that hard work always pays off, simply didn't possess a single noticeable acting skill.

"If only I could get a piece of film on myself, I know I could crack the nut," he would say with a relentless Billy Budd optimism you knew was only prelude to another round of heartache and rejection.

Or maybe not.

On February 17, 1981, at ten thirty in the morning, Dave called me with stunning news.

"Bob, I'm inviting you and the whole gang to a world premiere of my first film. I've got several good scenes in the picture, and would like your advice as to which ones I could put on an audition reel to finally get an agent."

"That's great news, Dave. Congratulations. I wouldn't miss it for the world. When and where, pal?"

"It's at the Aero this Saturday at 9:00. Eh, some folks are going formal, but a business suit would be fine."

Two days later an impressive gold gilded invitation arrived with directions to a movie theater buried in the back streets of Santa Monica.

But, wait a minute. The invite said 9 AM. That can't be. No production company in the world premieres its film at 9:00 in the morning…on a Sunday.

It must have been a misprint.

It wasn't.

I arrived at 8:30, and walked right into a Fellini dream sequence with a touch of red-tag sales days thrown in. A nearby Methodist Church choir was belting out "Jesus Is The Answer" loud enough to provide a comically blasphemous mismatched musical backdrop for the tacky dementia unfolding in front of the theater.

A service man in overalls leaning against a giant searchlight was trying to convince a short, fat guy in a Scotch plaid tuxedo that it made no sense to turn on a million candlepower zeon lamp in broad daylight. He lost. The useless beam was turned on, and quickly burned off several dry branches of an overhead maplethorpe.

The "first nighter" crowd was less than two dozen, mostly friends, relatives, and cast members in typical eclectic L.A. streetwear, meaning brushed corduroy jackets over Che Guevera T-shirts, no socks, and the mandatory over-exuberant glad-handing buzz. A few were in improvised imitation formal chic. All were concentrating their attention on a colorful array of heavily rouged, middle-aged vixens exposing ample areas of their obviously reconstructed breasts. All were toasting one another with plastic champagne glasses. A disinterested hiccupping midget dressed as a jockey, holding two large cardboard plates filled with scrawny little clumps of brown and green stuff, was passing among the group having no luck unloading his mysterious cargo.

The Aero Theater, a crumpling memory to past glory days when crushed red velvet and gold leaf Egyptian symbols were the height of art nouveau, was now living on the kindness of strangers who hired her out for birthday parties, bar mitzvahs, graduation night hijinks, and occasional low-budget film screenings.

The smog-damaged marquee had lost a fifty-year battle with L.A.'s notorious tormentor, and had turned into a giant blackboard, cracked in a dozen places, which lent little glamour to the words, "World Premiere Today".

The hand-written note on the front door erased it altogether.

"Bathrooms Out Of Order.
If You Have To Go, Do It Now!"

Dave was nervous as he ushered several of the old gang into the theater to the accompaniment of the musical Methodists now "Bringing In The Sheaves." "Thanks for coming. I really appreciate it. I really do. I've reserved a row for us right in the middle."

We made small talk about the old days and exchanged looks that beamed hope our old persevering friend would finally break through and achieve his goal of "getting a good piece of film" on himself.

In the middle of the pre-curtain speech by the short, fat producer in the Scotch plaid tuxedo, Dave leaned toward all of us and apologetically whispered, "I guess I should have told you all that this is, eh, a kind of exploitative film." He was quick to add, "But not pornographic. At least, that's what I was told. So if you see anything, you know, distasteful, try to overlook it and just concentrate on my part, which is straight dramatic acting. I guarantee you."

The opening sequence was considerably less than straight dramatic acting.

A voluptuous naked female swimming underwater rushed toward an equally naked male swimmer on the surface to the familiar staccato thrum of the most effective scary music score of all time.

"Da dum, da dum, da dum, dum. dum, dum, dum...."

The crescendo built as the female came up from underneath the unsuspecting male swimmer, opened her mouth, and with a thunderous climatic downbeat was about to perform submerged oral sex on the happy victim above, when the title exploded on screen, "Deep Jaws."

Poor Dave, stunned and humiliated, repeated over and over, "I had no idea. I had no idea. Oh, my God."

The old gang is halfway between laughter and sadness—laughter at the absurdity of attending a world premiere of a porno flick in semi-formal attire on a Sunday morning, and sadness at the monumental embarrassment of a sincere friend desperately hoping to break the endless cycle of the actor's futile struggle for acceptance and finally break into the movies.

Dave sat motionless with his head bowed for the first fifteen minutes of a film whose only purpose was to find multiple angles to exult breast implants.

There was a plot of sorts. A struggling Hollywood producer, played by Dave, hoodwinks the U.S. Army Signalman's Corps into advancing him money to produce training films. Instead, he makes a porno film in hopes of making more money, which will finally allow him to finance the artistic movie that will legitimize him as a bona fide Hollywood producer.

A miraculous birth begins.

Three scenes into the movie, a fully clothed Dave appeared. A lifetime of terminal shyness, awkward self consciousness, and a laundry list of doubts have suddenly disappeared. In their place is a strong, confident surprisingly effective presence on screen. Each scene begins the same.

A tight shot of Dave exuding his newly found strength for three or four seconds and then a pull back to a wider shot revealing one or more of the heavily rouged ladies either jiggling their Mount Rushmore size assets or bending over to display the dental floss thong separating their silky smooth buttocks, thus erasing any possibility of editing it out for Dave's audition piece of film.

His dying spirit is momentarily reprieved after each scene as all of us reach across the row to pat him on the back with genuine praise for his truly startling transformation into a believable film actor.

Halfway through the movie, Dave grabs my arm and is two octaves above a whisper when he says, "Here it is, Bob. Here comes my big office scene.

No women, no nudity, just me and a confrontation with the Army General and his aides. It's a powerful scene and I think I did a great job. I'm sure we can splice this out for my reel."

It is, indeed, a powerful scene. Dave is true grit strong-jawed Rambo tough in putting down the U.S. Army threat, and he was right. There were no women or any trace of nudity. That is, there weren't any when the scene was originally shot. But Dave Engleman's world would be forever changed by the special effects wizardry of movie making.

Unbeknownst to our long-suffering friend, when his defining moment was at hand, the cameraman panned sufficiently left to leave a wide expanse of unoccupied blue screen showing. The effect is called chroma-key, and it is used to superimpose another piece of film in that background.

As the veins in Dave's neck swelled and throbbed in dramatic intensity when he pounded the desk and drove home his dialogue like a passionate advocate pleading a first amendment case before the Supreme Court, the post-production editors back in the producer's garage, had added some window dressing to the drama. Literally. Framed in the window over the inspired Dave's left shoulder appeared a a young blond, blue-eyed stud on a scaffold. He proceeded to wash the window in slow, purposeful movements. Seconds later, as Dave, in the foreground, arms extended like a crucified Christ was delivering crushing emotional blows to his adversaries, a naked lady was lowered upside down by her feet right in front of the delighted window washer. Her upside down head was conveniently positioned at his midsection. She proceeded to unzip his pants and, well, the rest was no surprise to anyone but poor Dave, who stood up temporarily blocking the projector feed to the screen and uttered a heartbreaking, "No, no, this is not right."

It wasn't, but that's what you get when you believe a porno producer in a plaid tuxedo who assures you he's hiring you for some fully clothed straight dramatic acting.

An already humble man was now reduced to complete mortification, but somehow was able to swallow his last shadow of pride and take the scene to every reputable post-production studio in Hollywood in an effort to find a process that could make the upside down hanging fellatio go away forever.

He found one, but he'd have to win the lottery to pay for the most difficult edit in screen history.

Dave Engleman never got his piece of film, nor did he ever get a single paying job as a professional actor. The check from the guy in the plaid tuxedo bounced. Nice guys may finish first in the movies, but in real life most dreamers go back to the nine to five world and live out their quiet lives of frustration in total anonymity. Dave went back to selling office supplies over the phone by day and attended acting classes at night as a non-paying observer.

Epilogue

In the murky irrational world of Hollywood make-believe, where the past is never prologue and anything is possible, Dave Engleman modified his dream. Two years later he opened his own acting school next to a Catholic bookstore in Burbank, California.

Four years later he bought a forty-foot sail boat and a Cessna 180 airplane to go along with his three-bedroom condo down the street from John Wayne in the exclusive part of Newport Beach.

Eight years later, the Hollywood Reporter Magazine named him the second most successful acting coach in the film capital of the world.

THEN THERE'S JUAN

He grew up in the old century.

Things were black and white back then, including the color of people's skin. Oh, sure he was brought up to treat people the way they treated you, but somehow you looked at people different from you in a, well, different way.

Now he's old and sees his country going to hell in a hand basket.

The different people come in all colors now, black, brown, red, yellow, and a whole lot in between—then there's Juan.

Lots of them sneak across the border, refuse to speak English, play loud music at night, have no idea what patriotism is, routinely cheat, lie, and swell our prisons with their drive-by violence—then there's Juan.

He can't help looking at graffiti, ignorance, dirty streets, and rude, crude behavior as the only legacy of the different people.

Just about everyone his age feels we'd all be better off if they'd all go back where they came from—then there's Juan.

Juan was seven years old, when he first met him at the neighborhood YMCA. Juan was part of the different people, but he smiled a lot and said, "Yes, sir" and "no, sir" and "please" and "thank you," and was always eager to learn.

The man liked that. He asked the boy, "Do you know your state capitals?"

The little boy scrunched up his face and thought about it for a few seconds "No, sir, I don't, but I could learn."

"Good," said the man, "because if you do, you'll be a very smart person and you'll remember them the rest of your life."

The man bought the boy a large map of the United States with the capitals of each state in great big red letters.

He said, "Just learn one new capital a day, and when I see you, I'll test you, Okay?" There were some days when the little boy would get the answer right, but there many more days he simply couldn't remember.

The man liked the smiling little boy's efforts, but figured, after all, he was like all the other different people who really didn't care about learning and becoming true Americans.

The little boy didn't come back to the Y for a very long time.

The man never forgot his smiling, happy, red-cheeked round face all full of hope and honest curiosity, and felt sad he would lose all that promise buried in the mediocrity of the different people with their rude, crude, ignorant culture.

As the years went by more and more of the different people arrived. They took over whole neighborhoods. Their different faces appeared everywhere on TV and the movies. They joined unions, went on strike for higher wages, demanded people who looked like them hold office to help run the country.

The man lost all hope in an America he'd once loved so deeply. "How could we have sold out our own country to these different people who don't give a damn about the history and values that made us so great," he thought so many times.

Then one day while working out at the Y in the middle of many different people speaking many different languages, his life changed forever.

A tall, good-looking young man with a little boy at his side approached him. Both had identical smiling, red-cheeked round faces and crew cuts.

They snapped to attention in unison and gave very smart salutes.

"Good morning, sir. It's me, Juan. I'm a U.S. Marine officer now, and this is my son, John F. Kennedy Gonzales. We have a surprise for you."

Right there amid the exercycles, the free weights, and the senior citizens' Healthy Heart aerobics class, Juan and little John started with Alabama and flawlessly proceeded to West Virginia naming all fifty capitals without pause or doubt. Right after, "Wyoming, Cheyenne," the seniors broke into enthusiastic applause followed by lots of high fives.

The man swelled with pride the way we all do when we feel we've made a small contribution to a valuable life, but it wasn't enough to erase his deep-seated distrust of the different people. That continued to November 29^t, 2003 at 5:15PM. That's when the Y director placed a notice with a picture of a smiling, young Marine officer on the large lobby bulletin board next to the American flag.

IN MEMORIUM

While rescuing two wounded fellow Marines under fire in an attack on his convoy in Mozul, Iraq, Second Lieutenant Juan Jose Gonzales, USMC, was shot and killed by unknown insurgents. Juan was a long time member of the Y, who coached pee wee basketball, taught civics classes, and was a five-time winner of the Community Service of the Year Award.

We are all diminished by the death of one person, but when the best among us is lost, we must pause in special tribute.

The old man never spoke of differences again.

APPOINTMENT ON
THE ROCK

Sir Arthur Thurston Twigg-Jones would be an imposing figure, even if my life wasn't about to end at his hands in just a few moments.

Well over six feet tall, ramrod straight with a stolid face chiseled from Gothic marble, and punctuated by a walrus mustache that ran east and west and then curled north and south. He was a magnificent relic of Kipling's faded imperialistic age, more suited to lead the Light Brigade into the valley of death than to command a few dozen soldiers and sailors of the British crown in a mere ceremonial function high on a rock at the mouth of the Mediterranean. His every movement was slow, measured, dramatic like the chilling apathy of a Roman centurion about to put a defeated enemy to the sword. Giants were coursing in his genes. Nelson at Trafalgar, Chinese Gordon at Khartoum, Kitchener surveying the Crimea. He was there.

Now he answered to First Lord of the Admiralty and Governor-General of Gibraltar.

Three hours ago, his paranoid antithesis, Captain Edward Jefferson Higgins, commanding officer of the troop attack transport, U.S.S. Telfair (APA 210), grabbed the ship's 1 MC announcing system and roared my name throughout the ship followed by, "Report to my cabin on the double, dammit"

A Bela Lugosi look-a-like survivor of three destroyers torpedoed out from under him in the Pacific seventeen years earlier, Captain H was blowing steam out of all his facial orifices.

"How long have you been a qualified officer of the deck, Mister?"

I knew enough not to reply. The career insomniac who saw every junior officer as a target of opportunity and often made his points by throwing pieces of his inscribed chinaware at where your head had just been was a natural Shakespearean as well. He only spoke in soliloquies, and had already recorded your answers long before you entered the room.

Your participation in mock conversations with him was limited to standing at attention and pretending to make eye contact, while actually staring at the crescent-shaped hairy mole at the base of his slightly hooked nose. I had mastered both strategies.

"Do you know what I'm holding here…yes, you're right…messages sent from this ship during your mid-watch, Lieutenant…all very proper and accurate…except this one…this time you've gone too far and you can kiss your naval career goodbye. Do you hear that? That's a limey helicopter about to land on our forecastle…and do you know why…because the British commander at Gibraltar read this message this morning and wants to see you immediately…and you can bet it's not to award you the Victoria Cross…your ass is grass, Mister, and once the admiral hears about it, heads are going to roll. Get out of here and on that chopper NOW!"

I better explain.

Since July 24,1704, when the Brits captured the 2.5 square miles of limestone rock at the western entrance to the Mediterranean, a seagoing tradition was born. All ships sailing into the eighteen-mile opening separating the southern tip of the Iberian Peninsula from the coast of North Africa were required to communicate by semaphore, flashing light, or radio transmission, asking permission to proceed through the straits from the tower atop the 1400 foot Rock of Gibraltar.

In smart military brevity, the tower would send a request for identification, usually, "What ship?", to which you must reply immediately with your ship's name. A mere formality, but one observed by the British with two centuries of flawless precision and pride.

It was 0200 hours on a beautiful Van Gogh starry, starry night on August 23,1962. The Telfair was the lead ship in a five-ship amphibious squadron formation. As the officer of the deck I was responsible for maintaining course, speed, and to accord all honors on behalf of the other ships. A heady, but totally enjoyable task for a hopeless romantic who missed out at victory at sea in World War II due to the fact the Navy had a strong bias against recruiting three year olds.

I could only imagine the dangers faced by my heroic predecessors in these historic straits as they zigzagged through mine fields and exchanged gunfire with deadly enemy dreadnaughts lying in wait.

But you can only fantasize so much on a long, boring watch that holds little opportunity to test your mettle in battle with a world at peace.

So you sing love songs of the forties, conduct surprise drills for your equally bored wheelhouse watch to keep them sharp, check your charts a hundred times an hour, use your land-based sense memory to remember what it was like to go to a bathroom and sit on a commode without twenty wisecracking dudes sitting elbow to elbow at the same time checking out your business and creating that insalubrious symphony of sounds ever present in such communal male facilities. When these preoccupations run thin, you perfect your seamanship skills by rehearsing in your mind all those actions that might earn you a combat decoration or two in time of conflict. I had single-handedly shot down two German Messerschmitt Bf 109s, out-maneuvered two approaching torpedoes, and had ex-tinguished a raging fire attacking the high explosives forward magazine when it happened.

At 0210, the Gibraltar tower picked up our squadron on a visual sighting and sent the traditional identifying message, "What ship?"

I had exhausted all my Bing Crosby favorites, drilled my bridge team to the point of near mutiny, and won the Navy Cross with two clusters. Back to mundane duties. I grabbed the port signal light and flashed out a response in Morse code.

A surprised first-class signalman standing nearby smiled and laconically intoned, "I think you just made history, sir."

What I made was trouble.

Now I stood at attention, surprisingly resigned to my fate as Sir Arthur puffed on a large panatela enjoying one of his signature long dramatic pauses. He had obviously dressed down many a junior officer in his time and relished the routine, perhaps more so, because this time there was a Yank walking the plank. The dismantlement began with a brief history lesson.

"I understand your Navy doesn't put much pride in tradition as we English do, but tradition, young man, has built and colonized the greatest empire the world has ever seen."

My Brooklyn redneck background was rushing to my tongue, and I was about to counter with, "Well, we had enough tradition to save your ass in two world wars, pal." I didn't. I figured I had raised the stress level of international relations high enough for one twenty-four hour period.

Lord Nelson blew smoke rings that nestled in my hair and slipped down the sides of my cheeks. His words now became tiny rapier thrusts calculated to inflict just enough pain to alert me of the final coup de grace aimed at my heart. "For 250 years we have been requiring all mariners passing The Rock to reply to our I.D. request, and for 250 years they have done so…until now."

I could feel the cold steel of his blade making its way past my left pectoral, ending my boyhood dreams of joining John Paul Jones, Dewey, Nimitz and Halsey in the pantheon of great naval heroes as well as having a stretch of the Brooklyn Belt Parkway named in my honor. Sir Arthur Hornblower, I'm sure, was about to recommend a general courts martial for gross insubordination, severe tradition deficit disorder and possible further humiliation forcing me to lay prostrate at the feet of the Queen Mum and make a public apology.

It didn't happen.

Instead, the First Lord of the Admiralty broke out in a raucous laugh that shook the four-bottle set of Dewars gin on his desk, and whacked my shoulders in a thunderclap of exuberance.

"Good show, Yank. Very inventive. Caught us all out of our jodhpurs, so to speak. God knows we need a spot of fun in this damnable routine."

He put his tree trunk right arm around me, squeezed my shoulder blades together with a crack, and bellowed, "You're our guest of honor tonight at dinner. Don't worry about your duties. I've cleared it all with your Admiral. We'll fly you back tomorrow. I'll have my staff join us."

He summoned instant magic by ringing a dainty little cow bell on his desk that must have been connected directly to Hollywood Central Casting. In they came, every charmingly stodgy character actor from all the 1930 black-and-white English movies I had ever seen. Basil Rathbone, C. Aubrey Smith, and good 'ol Doctor Watson, Nigel Bruce, were soon insisting we remain on a first-name basis throughout the evening.

That wonderful absurdly momentous night high above the glistening Mediterranean, I was gleefully thrust center stage with the bigger-than-life cast of H.M.S. Pinafore, ceremonial relics in puffy white uniforms with over-sized medals, waxed mustaches, Elizabethan diction, and a limitless capacity to drink three different kinds of alcohol in the same glass and remain conscious. I sat at the head of a three hundred year old oak table once used by Charles I during legendary debaucheries. If Charlie's guests dined on the same justifiably maligned English cuisine we were being served, I can understand why they skipped dessert and went straight to the kinky menu. Puffy green stuff, chunky yellow stuff, meat from unknown parts of a lamb all covered in orange sauce as tasteless as corn starch on dehydrated liver. But whada-hell, I had avoided the firing squad and was back on the fast track to an honorable discharge.

We all sang bawdy barracks ditties from three wars, toasted every English king in history with wine from Sir Arthur's private stash, and vigorously debated the comparable lust quotient of American and Brit-ish females.

I flew back to my ship the next morning with a gigantic post-wino binge headache, an autographed picture of the First Lord of the British Admiralty, and two cases of Hannigan's Tiger Beer for my hopelessly confused Captain.

All this for two simple words flashed through a midsummer's night.

At 0210 Greenwich Mean Time, the high command on Gibraltar signaled, "What Ship?"

I flashed back, "What rock?"

FORTY-TWO
MINUTES WITH THE
BOYS OF PEARL

Author's note:

From December 1-7, 2001, five hundred survivors of the Japanese attack on Pearl Harbor gathered in Honolulu for the sixtieth anniversary commemoration. Lectures, open forums with prominent historians, and eyewitness accounts occupied the first six days, along with testimonial dinners and tours of historic places that figured prominently in that day of infamy. The seventh day saw thousands gather on, in, and around the Arizona Memorial for a day of stunningly emotional remembrance. But the greater meaning of the event could only be absorbed by simply walking up and chatting with the survivors, "the boys of Pearl." Here are my unedited notes of one such encounter with history.

2:50 PM: Old reliable Bill picked me up at the Honolulu airport precisely on time. I've never known him to be late for anything in the thirty-seven years we've known one another.

"Aloha, shipmate. We're all set up in the VIP section on December 7 at the boat landing. Couldn't get onboard the Memorial; that's reserved for the Arizona survivors, their families, and military brass."

3:17 PM: Bill drops me off at my Waikiki hotel.

"Say, what hotels are the boys staying at during all the festivities?" I ask.

"I think the Ala Moana has the largest batch, then the Holiday Inn, Hale Koa at (Fort) DeRussy, and the rest are spread out all over the place. Why?"

I don't have to answer that. He knows as well as I. We both joined the Navy at the same time. We both served as officers at Pearl, where saluting the sunken Arizona every day was the highlight of the day for two four-year-old neighborhood kids who fought WW II in cardboard helmets and broomstick rifles.

These were and always would be our heroes. This was their last hurrah.

3:24 PM: Call the concierge at the Ala Moana Hotel.

"Can you tell me if there are any events planned today in your hotel for the Pearl Harbor Survivors' group?"

"I don't know of any activities, sir, but there's a whole lot of them sitting around the lobby right now waiting for the buses to take them to a dinner or something."

3: 45 PM: Arrive at the lobby—clusters of old men, many in wheelchairs, with walkers or using canes, all in white campaign hats with blue piping with names of legendary ships emblazoned on one side, U.S.S. Oklahoma BB 37, U.S.S. Pennsylvania BB 38, U.S.S. Utah BB 31, and dozens of miniature battle ribbons on the other side. The din of high spirited remembrances compete with the Christmas carols over the loud speakers. Unconcerned wives in comfortable shoes seem more interested in the holiday decorations than the living history unfolding. A Japanese tour group wearing large white name tags with a red ball in the center, mill around the periphery, unaware of the irony of their presence. A few kids are doing a bad job of pretending to admire the large gingerbread houses around the twenty-foot Christmas tree in the center, while stealthily chipping off pieces to eat. A frail lady in a plain yellow dress is sitting alone at the far side of the room holding a framed picture of a smiling young sailor. She carefully observes the ship names on the caps as the men saunter back and forth.

Suddenly, a tap on the shoulder. I turn and am greeted with a farm-fresh smile from a plump lady in a pea-green muumuu with a red, white and blue scarf with the words, "*United We Stand*" draped over her right shoulder.

"Pardon me, sir, you wouldn't be a survivor of the battleship Pennsylvania by any chance?"

"No, ma'am, I'm not. About the only thing I've survived is sixteen years of Catholic school." She smiles and starts to walk away.

"What information are you looking for? Perhaps I can help."

"I'm hoping to find someone who knew my brother. He was one of the fifteen sailors killed when a bomb hit the ship in dry dock."

She's Norman Rockwell's kindly, concerned country schoolmarm, but with an obvious touch of sadness.

"His body was never recovered. I was only four years old on Pearl Harbor Day so I never really got to know him. I was hoping maybe some men from the ship might be here who knew him and could tell me something about him. I promised our mom before she died a few years ago that I would find someone. This is pretty much my last chance to do that."

She holds up a picture of a young smiling sailor in a similar pose as the one being held by the lady in the yellow dress across the room.

"His name was John Condon, Firemen First Grade, Engineering Division. We're from Iowa."

"I'll keep my eyes peeled for Pennsylvania sailors and let you know."

"Thank you. That would be very kind of you." She smiles and sits back on the big plumeria-colored couch alongside an overweight gent in an art deco hot-pink aloha shirt, the kind your teenager daughter calls retro-chic.

"I'm Fred, her husband. I was in the Korean War. We don't have reunions. Hell, nobody cares about the ones you didn't win."

The other roly-poly next to him chimes in, "Yeah, ya' never see John Wayne in A Korean War movie, do ya'?" They poke one another playfully and laugh. "Aren't these characters something?" says the buxom grandma with a flaming hibiscus in her hair. "They arrived a few days ago old men who could hardly walk and talk, and now look at them. They think they're young again, horsing around, lying about all the women they thought they had. It's really something."

"Whatdoyamean, 'think they had', says her wheelchair-bound husband in a U.S.S. California cap and taking deep breaths from his portable oxygen tank. "Whatdayathink put me in this chair?" More laughter.

4:01 PM: I start cluster-hopping, introducing myself as a writer and former Navy Public Affairs Officer in the early sixties. My acceptance is easy and immediate. The little kid inside is one of the boys with his heroes, listening, observing, and collecting signatures on his limited edition, official Pearl Harbor 60th Anniversary poster with the title, *A Day To Remember, A Time Not Forgotten.*

Another wife shakes her head in disbelief, "Boy, Alzheimer's doesn't have a chance here. These guys all of a sudden remember everything. Amazing."

The stocky man in the U.S.S. Oklahoma cap chirps in, "What's so amazing about it? I drop you right in the middle of hell before breakfast and see if you don't remember it the rest of your life. The mind takes a picture of events that are, eh, what's that word again, Earl?"

"Traumatic," says the thin man with the stone-faced grin in the U.S.S. Utah cap, "You know, like your wedding day." More laughter as his wife playfully whacks him over the head with her *Hawaii, Isle of Golden Dreams* shopping bag and zings him with," Yeah. Well for me, buster, it was our wedding *night.*"

4:07 PM: A small, neatly dressed Japanese man in a dark suit and baseball cap is signing posters and posing for group pictures with some of the boys. He has an ageless face with a permanent smile that comes dangerously close to a smirk. I'm curious. I get closer and read the writing on his white cap with the red ball in the middle, "WW II Zero Pilots' Association." Five survivors of the 371 planes who dove from the skies in the early morning sunshine of December 7, 1941, and forced America into the bloodiest war in history are in attendance. Chinichi Kurosawa is one of them.

In the let bygones be bygones atmosphere when old men who share history gather, the line between friend and foe is usually washed away by the resignation of age. Eighty and ninety-year-old warriors on medication tend not to hold grudges, even for unprovoked sneak attacks. But it's also obvious the monumental horror of the event that bonded these men from both sides would forever keep a part of them frozen in yesterday.

Boys again, seventeen and eighteen, in the middle of an opening act to a reign of blood and terror that would claim fifty million lives in battles fought on six of the seven continents and would change their fate and the life of the planet forever. Here they were, the arthritic remnants of the defining moment in their nation's life. They were fading living history, a closing chapter, and they knew it. Scattered among these amiable old salts were two Congressional Medals of Honor, seven Navy Crosses, and a thousand stories of heroism that would never be told. But they didn't make a big deal of it. They left that to others, others who would call them "The Greatest Generation" for saving the world from evil by drawing on simple character, and an uncanny everyday blue collar courage to get the job done no matter what.

They were good-natured old geezers now in mismatched shirts and slacks, more interested in a good belly laugh than a trip down memory lane. Oh, sure, they'd tell you their stories, where they were and what they saw when the bombs fell, but not out of ego. Never ego. It was something else, much deeper.

I asked the man with the crippled left arm and two Purple Heart pins on his U.S.S. Oklahoma cap just what is it? Like all his unpretentious peers in the room, he spoke in straight lines, from gut to mouth to your ears. "Gratitude and a lot of guilt, I think," he said.

"I understand the gratitude part, but what's the guilt?" I asked.

"Jackie Delahanty, Pipefitter Third Class. God, I can see his big Irish mug right now. My best buddy. We did everything together. A couple of torpedoes hit us, the ship turns over, and we're trapped for three days up to our neck in dirty, oily water, dead bodies, and smoke. We finally pry open a hatch, but I'm too weak to make it through, so he holds it open with one hand and pushes me through with his other. I make it out. He falls back and drowns. They give me a medal, and I get a chance to grow old. Why? I think all the guys here have a Jackie Delahanty they carry around in their minds every day. A guy who never got a chance to fall in love, get married, buy a house, take the kids to a ballgame. Ya' know, all the things we're supposed to do."

He smiles, almost apologetically.

"I know it sounds corny, but ya' ask 'why them and not me?' "And you never get an answer. I guess we come back, each in his own way, ya' know, to say thank you for the gift and kinda hope we lived a good enough life to deserve it." He pauses, putting his good hand to his chin, rerunning in his mind what he just said.

"Yeah, that's it. We're all here to say 'thank you' one last time.

His agitated wife in the big straw sun hat breaks the mood.

"Well, if those damn tour buses don't arrive soon to take us to dinner, we're all going to be able to thank the guys who didn't make it, in person, because we're going to starve to death."

4:10 PM: Chinichi was now signing posters without being asked. The boy in the Arizona cap moved his hand over the poster, indicating the Zero pilot's signature was not welcome.

"Not mine, thank you," he said, firmly, without bitterness.

His wife chided him, "What are you doing? The man wants to sign your poster, Harold. Let him."

"No, dammit!" His abrupt reply overpowered Gene Autry's *Here Comes Santa Claus* and halted all conversations beyond. All eyes turned to the two men. Even the Howangii Japanese Tour Group pressed the pause button.

The Arizona sailor took a moment to read the pilot's name tag, then spoke slowly, softly, again without malice.

"You understand English, Lieutenant Kurosawa?"

"Yes, I do," came the immediate reply.

Unaware the entire lobby population was frozen in stunned silence watching him, the Arizona survivor continued, pointing to his poster on the side table. "You see these words here. That's the theme of this anniversary. 'American-Japanese Reconciliation.' But in sixty years you folks still haven't apologized for what you did. Don't you think it's about time?"

Wow! Another bomb had just fallen on the Pearl Harbor story.

A hundred fifty people took deep breaths at the same time and sucked out all the air on the ground floor of the Ala Moana Hotel. Nothing moved. Even cowboy Gene's voice seemed to drop down to a whisper. Slowly, imperceptibly at first, Imperial Japanese fighter pilot, Chinichi Kurosawa took two steps backward, lowered his eyes, and bowed ceremoniously toward the Arizona sailor. His fellow countrymen on the other side of the lobby in the tour group, unaware of the significance of the gesture, took their cue from him and bowed in unison. Still bend over in respect, he offered, "On behalf of my country, I offer my sincere apology."

Wow! What a moment in unwritten history.

Throughout the six previous days of pomp and ceremony, various representatives of the Japanese had made speeches, laid wreaths, presented plaques, and raised their sake cups in mutual toasts, but whether for purposes "of saving face" or some other reason lost in the confusing affairs of nations, carefully avoided an apology, until now.

Pin-drop silence soon turned to nervous laughter as a faint, "Holy shit!" rose from somewhere.

A blind veteran in a U.S.S. West Virginia cap blurted out, "Will someone tell me whatdahell is going on?"

He apparently was hard of hearing, too. His wife leaned over and responded loud enough to clear the room of any tension and break the ice for good.

"The war is officially over now. We can all go home."

More laughter, robust, unforced, and meaningful.

Hubby hasn't heard a thing.

"Is that the damn tour buses? Damn, I'm hungry." Historic moments are short-lived in this crowd.

The Arizona sailor and the attacking pilot sign one another's posters and introduce their families. The smile on Chinichi's face is undeniably genuine now.

Gene is back in the saddle again.

"Here Comes Santa Claus, here home Santa Claus, right down Santa Claus Lane…"

4:15 PM: The Iowa lady is sitting attentively in the middle of three men all wearing U.S.S. Pennsylvania caps. She's learning about the brother she never knew, and it must be very good. The group conversation is punctuated frequently by laughter and animated gestures that keep her smiling broadly. Soon the men stand.

One barks out, "A-ten-hut!" Old habits return. They respond in smart military fashion. She holds up her picture of the smiling young sailor. His former shipmates ignore a variety of ailments, as previously bent bodies straighten up and honor him with a picture perfect sharp salute. Soon others sense the moment. Spontaneously, without direction, the boys of Pearl, one by one, abandon conversations, wheelchairs, walkers and canes, stand and join the salute to a fallen comrade they never knew. It is neither sentimental nor posed. It is simply a pure moment of love understood more deeply by the brotherhood of old men who have survived the crucible of war.

Soon everyone is applauding. The Iowa lady is smiling through her tears, "Thank you, thank you, everyone. You are all very special people."

4:17 PM: The frail lady in the yellow dress holding her picture is now sobbing openly. She is being consoled by two strapping young men who bear a strong resemblance to the sailor in the picture. I walk over and explain to them how the Iowa lady found shipmates of her loved one and, perhaps, they, too, will have the same luck.

The taller of the men is a gentle giant with a soft voice. "This is my dad, George Eugene Roe. He was a survivor, a gunner's mate aboard the Tennessee. He never missed one of these reunions. He always came by himself, so we promised him we'd all come with him this time. He died two weeks ago, but we kinda figure he's here with us."

4:18 PM: A TV network reporter is interviewing the blind veteran. He's expecting a dramatic, personal, detailed account of the day that changed the sailor's life forever. He doesn't get it. "Tell me, sir, what is your most vivid memory of what happened aboard the battleship West Virginia that day?"

"It sunk. Say, do you see any tour buses outside? They're supposed to take us to dinner."

4:19 PM: Over by the Christmas tree, another TV reporter is roaming around looking for a story. He spots a young girl and her mother with matching September 11, 2001, remembrance ribbons pinned to their blouses. He cautiously moves a microphone in front of the girl and asks, "What does Pearl Harbor mean to you?" She scrunches her face and says, "What's Pearl Harbor?"

4:20 PM: Both camera crews are missing the biggest reunion story of the seven-day event.

I walk over to a small group of vets and their wives sitting under a large display of suspended poinsettias framing a colorful Hawaiian greeting, "Mele Kalikimaka and Hauoli Makahiki Hou (Merry Christmas and Happy New Year).

Two men, both wearing U.S.S. Maryland BB 46 caps, are sitting opposite one another playing a hand of poker. Shipfitter Third Class, Lyle Giettesbrough, is Jimmy Stewart thin, with the same self-effacing manner. Quartermaster striker, Elton Brattlee, is what you'd imagine

Spanky of Our Gang Comedy would look like when he's drawing social security checks—a contented grin on a fire-hydrant torso with a liberal touch of mischief-maker showing every time he opens his mouth. Jimmy Stewart discards two cards. Spanky objects.

"Wait a minute, you can't ask for two cards. You already drew two," says Elton.

"What are you talking about? The game just begun, don't you remember," replies Lyle.

Back and forth they trade jibes, while their wives shake their heads, repeating the same sentence over and over.

"Nobody's going to believe this. Nobody."

Now, the story that never made it to the network news.

At 0754, December 7, 1941, Lyle and his best friend, Elton, were doing what they always did on their duty-free Sunday morning; playing poker for a penny a hand on the fantail of the Maryland, moored alongside the Oklahoma at Battleship Row off Ford Island. Depending upon who you believe, they had just dealt a hand and were considering their play when a 1700-pound bomb crashed through five decks of the nearby Arizona. The concussion flung Lyle forty feet in the air and landed him in the oil-soaked flaming waters of the harbor.

"I remember looking back at the Maryland and seeing the fantail in a blazing fireball. I started crying. I knew nobody could have survived that inferno. Elton had to be dead. I was dragged up on Ford Island, and spent a few months in a hospital recovering before they assigned me to another ship. I went through every major campaign in the Pacific. When I got home, I called an old friend on the Maryland, and he confirmed everybody aft of frame 138 was killed that day, and I was the lucky one. I even had a memorial mass said for Elton."

At 3:30 PM, just a few minutes ago, an old Spanky McFarland in his bright U.S.S. Maryland cap walked under the Mele Kalikimaka sign and heard someone yell, "Elton, Elton Brattlee, is that you?"

"My God, Lyle, Lyle, is that you, buddy. I thought you were dead."

"My wife has been telling me that for years."

They hugged, they cried, they slapped hands, and hugged some more.

Seems Elton was thrown off the fantail, too, but on the other side, and spent six months in Tripler Army Hospital, in the hills above Pearl Harbor, recouping before being sent to the Atlantic to fight Nazis. Neither man had ever attended a single Maryland reunion, nor had they ever returned to Pearl since that deadly Sunday.

Right in the middle of a hug, Elton says, "Wait a minute, don't go away. I'll be right back. He left and came back a few minutes later with a deck of Bicycle playing cards, compliments of the front desk.

"We're going to finish that game, because I was beating your fanny pretty good."

"What are you talking about? I was holding the best hand I ever had."

The reunited sailors each took the cards out of the deck they were holding back when they were eighteen-year-old shipmates on the most fateful day of the twentieth century. They then proceeded to complete the game they started sixty years ago.

Both were grinning ear to ear when Lyle spoke, "I call. Whatday-agot?"

Elton dropped his hand on the table, "Royal Flush, hearts. Where's my penny?"

"Not so fast, cowboy." Lyle drops his hand, "Royal Flush, clubs."

Their laughter ruffles the overhead poinsettias and infects the entire room.

"My God, Lyle, we're both as big at cheating as we were back then."

"Yeah, some things just never change," says a grinning Elton.

Their wives continue the litany now chanted by many more around them, "Nobody is going to believe this. Nobody."

4:22 PM: "Excuse me, young man," said the small, thin lady in the daisy dress.

"Would you be kind enough to take a picture of me and my husband by the Christmas tree?"

Bob and Viola Schneider, both 83, were dead ringers for the classic, American Gothic, pleasant stoics, rail thin, plain, with the undistinguishable features of the aging Everyman and Everywoman. It was no stretch at all to see them both in blue denim overalls, working a plow, bringing in a crop, or sitting quietly on a summer porch watching the fireflies dance in the afterglow of a sunset. We used to call such folks, "salt of the earth." It still seems appropriate.

We sat together for a few minutes in silent conversation. Both were painfully shy. Bob's Survivor's cap said, "1st Artillery Battery, Camp Malakole, Hawaii." Viola leaned over and whispered in my ear, "Bob doesn't talk much, but maybe you can find some information from this." She handed me a neatly folded old brown cardboard scrap book. A faded yellow newspaper clipping fell out. It was a front-page story from the *North County California Times*. The headline read, "Local Vet Recalls His Fighting Family."

The meek man with the pleasing, genuine smile scanning the room and quietly enjoying the playful banter of comrades comes from a long line of patriots.

Grandpa fought at Bull Run, Daddy was a career Army man who rode with Black Jack Pershing chasing Pancho Villa across the border. Bob and his two brothers were serving in and around Pearl during the attack. Two survived. Brother Lee, a waist gunner, crashed and died in a B-17 bomber. Dozens of old fading photos of smiling young boys standing next to giant artillery pieces pointed skyward. Dark-skinned island girls in hula skirts, Diamond Head, and Waikiki in carefree days before the war changed the landscape forever. And a letter written on personal stationary and addressed to the Pearl Harbor Survivors Association: "Your accomplishments in defense of liberty will never be forgotten, and America's debt to you will remain far more than we can ever repay." Signed, George Bush, President of the United States.

Bob broke a long silence. Turning to his wife of sixty-three years, he spoke softly, matter of fact, not bothering to emphasize one word over another.

"It's a wonderful reunion. We won't be around for the next one." She agreed. He turned back to all the activity around him, paused for a breath and continued, "I guess most of the fellas won't be either."

The three of us just sat there content to appreciate the boisterous camaraderie of a final chapter.

Bob broke the silence. "Funny, all of a sudden, I feel old."

4:30 PM: An excited vet in a U.S.S. Downes cap bursts through the main entrance and bellows, "Chow time."

The damned buses have finally arrived. Old legs suddenly have new life. In a few minutes, the lobby is empty. Two wheelchairs, three canes, one walker and a faded brown scrap book are absentmindedly abandoned.

The boys of Pearl are gone.

THE MOST IMPORTANT BUTTON IN THE WORLD

There are buttons that launch giant missiles of destruction.
    There are buttons that bring the world's greatest music to our ears.
    There are buttons that reduce the unknowable.
    There are buttons that attach.
    There are buttons that open.
    There are buttons that close.
    There are buttons that adorn.
    There are buttons that bring the planet to our fingertips.
    There are buttons that begin magic and wonder.
    There are buttons that end it.
    There are buttons that sustain life.
    There are buttons that finish it.
    All that we are and all that we can be has a button to push.

But the most important button of all, the one with all the answers, all the hope, all the possibilities, lies deep within the human console and is rarely pushed at all.

I'll push it now to consider my ending to this tale

....

....

Nothing came that rhymes, but that's all right.

I'm always a better me when I press the pause button, don't you agree?

BOB C, ED
SULLIVAN, AND ME

Thursday, January 15
11:15 AM

Bob Corso and I were young together.

Forty years ago we wore Buster Brown collars and silly bellboy uniforms in the middle of the greatest show business fantasy of the era. We were CBS ushers at the number one TV program in the universe, the Ed Sullivan Show. Every Sunday at 6:00 PM during rehearsals at Studio 52 at fifty-second and Broadway, we walked casually among the brightest stars in the firmament, legends who called us by our first names and occasionally sat down and chatted with us as if we were equals. Martin and Lewis, Frank Sinatra, Jimmy Durante, Burns and Allen, Jack Benny, Eddie Cantor, Henry Fonda, Clark Gable, Mae West, and Betty Davis. We got them double-decker ham and cheese on rye at the fabled Stage Door delicatessen. We changed their quarters into two dimes and a nickel so they could call their agents and demand more money on their next Hollywood blockbuster. We listened attentively, like courtiers around a throne, as they complained about their small dressing rooms and lack of VIP seating for their friends and lovers. We watched in the wings as they flubbed their lines, cursed the gods, and fought with the director for better lighting during dress rehearsals.

We sat with them in more privileged intimate moments during breaks, as they freely recounted the inside stories of their mythic journeys to immortality—great stories their audiences would never hear. Tales of monumental early struggles against a world that gave them no credit for talent and no hope for recognition. We devoured every impossibility, for we knew it would all end in storybook triumph, and if we were lucky, a whopper of a punch line just the way Bob and I hoped it would. You see, we were both taking the first steps to joining the immortals, and laughter was our common language.

We were actors in the golden age of New York theater. The Actors Studio right around the corner was the center of that universe. Brando, Dean, Monroe, Montgomery Clift, and every other marquee performer in the business was at arm's length everywhere you turned: sitting at the counter at Mindy's eating cheese Danish, just like us; coffee klatching at Junior's Restaurant at the corner of forty-seventh, analyzing dialogue and fueling the biggest acting-style revolution in the history of the art, hailing a cab on Broadway; or waiting patiently in our audience for the toast of the town, Ed Sullivan, to confer the royal imprimatur propelling them to a new height of celebrityhood by simply introducing them to everyone who owned a TV set in the Eisenhower years.

Miracles were commonplace for Bob and me.

Laurence Olivier called me up to his tiny dressing room on the second floor and asked, "Would you be kind enough to hold book while I recite?" Odin had come down from Valhalla and was asking me to help him memorize the soliloquies of Henry IV, Part 2.

Outside, Bob was laughing with Jerry Lewis, assuring him his pratfalls would go over big with our audience. In a few minutes I'd be the sole protector of two of our nation's most treasured icons carrying Charlie McCarthy and his rustic sidekick, Mortimer Snerd, in two very plain brown leather suitcases up to Edgar Bergen's corner dressing room next to Maurice Chevalier's, where he would be asking Bob to help him iron his favorite blue dress shirt with ruffles on the sleeves. We walked among the gods for a year and a half; Cary Grant, John Wayne, Red Skelton, Kate Smith, Paul Muni, and Bob Hope all called us by our first names. Our confidence was unshakable. We had been ordained. They were already making room for our statues in the Pantheon. *Making it* was a mere formality, nevertheless, we fortified our certain fate with acting, dancing, and singing classes, hundreds of auditions, and appearances in a dozen off-off and way off-Broadway productions in cold cellars, storefronts, garages, and one five-week run of Stalag 17 on a rooftop of an abandoned brassier factory three zip codes away on Staten Island. Nothing would deter us. After all, hadn't we seen our future? Hadn't we even picked out our seats in Ed's audience when the time came that the king-maker himself would introduce us as the two new brightest stars on The Great White Way?

It was an exhilarating time of uninterrupted dreaming for two unstoppable nineteen-year old warriors who saw all defeats as mere preface to glory.

Bob stayed in New York, always in hot pursuit. More acting lessons, more auditions, more shows, but always in the shadows of the great theaters, usually in a run-down second-story loft with a cast that outnumbered the audience. But he was good, real good. Many on both sides of the footlights agreed he had the undeniable predictor of acting success. He had *that certain something* every time he walked on stage. One critic even likened him to a young Anthony Quinn. It would only be a matter of time.

I hit the road in the dusty backwaters of the southwest with touring shows, summer stock, and a traveling version of the Oberammergau Passion Play in the role of Judas, betraying the Son of God twice a day and three times on Saturday.

Eventually I made it to Hollywood, did a few movies in forgettable roles, dozens of commercials, and enough appearances in series TV in the golden 70's to buy a house with two fireplaces, a pool, and an imitation marble birdbath.

Bob and I lost track of one another for several years, until one rainy day on Vine Street opposite the ABC Studios. I had just been rejected for a small but significant part in a Movie-of-the-Week Civil War drama starring an old one day acquaintance of mine way back when, Sir Lawrence Olivier. At the audition, I reminded him of our brief encounter with Henry IV, Part II, and was greeted with a cold, blank stare.

I was indulging my defeat as I passed a bareheaded chap in a rumpled raincoat humming a bouncy tune at the bus stop.

"Bob Corso, howyadoin,' pal?"

Either from pride or some ancient fear shared by all minstrels that by confessing to bad times you condemn yourself to repeat them, actors, even the best of friends, never answer that one truthfully.

"Doing real good promoting records but, you know, just to keep some caviar on the table for my wife and three daughters until I land some parts. I'm up for a couple of biggies."

He dug in to his well-worn black leather attache case with the masking tape around the handle and produced a thick pile of papers.

"Been doing a lot of writing, too. Finished three scripts and a great idea for a sitcom. It's gotta sell." Of course, it never did.

We laughed, we reminisced, and we held up the 91 bus as we hugged goodbye and made our old New York actor's salute—clenched fist against the heart accompanying it with "Never quit."

The next time I saw Bob he had three seconds of screen time as one of Don Corleone's bodyguards in the wedding scene of "The Godfather." No lines, but once again, he was close to the immortals.

The small parts got smaller and eventually disappeared in a town where talent, drive, and an undaunted sense of optimism count less than a grilled cheese on pumpernickel.

Bob's dreaming and constant dancing on the edge of financial abyss cost him his marriage, but not his hope. He became a house painter, a very good one, but only to finance more sitcom writing, more acting classes, more showcase performances for secretaries of agents and producers who didn't have the time to look at aging dreamers. Soon Bob opened a new corner of his relentless creativity, song writing. He wrote hundreds. Got friends to produce them in their living room studios and shopped them from Nashville to Beverly Hills. For reasons known only to the fickle ways of the Muse, not one project was accepted. Daily courage in small doses is the stuff of true artists. Bob C never let any of it dim the light behind his hope.

My light, however, flickered and died. I left acting fifteen years ago and transferred my need to perform to the stages of corporate America's conventions and business meetings, where I assumed the role of motivating speaker and trainer. It's been the longest run in my show biz career, but I know the play has run its course. I'm thinking about that certainty as I sit opposite Bob in the middle booth of our favorite once-a-year rendezvous site, Marie Callender's Restaurant on Riverside Drive in Toluca Lake, across the street from a popular sound recording studio and right next door to a major L.A. theater. Once again, we're surrounded by bright stars; Garry Marshall, Ron Howard, Bob Hope and his wife in the next booth, and a half-dozen scruffy long-haired scarecrows everyone under thirty recognizes as the new kings of heavy metal. We have no idea who they are.

Bob gestures enthusiastically with his paint-splattered hands, as he makes plans to revise his latest song, "Whatever Happened to the U.S. of A?" a powerful wake-up call to an America that has lost its way. All who hear it are instantly moved to applause and tears and earnestly proclaim the same praise, "That song has got to be a hit."

The music industry has never returned one of Bob's calls.

His persistent belief in fairy-tale endings where the best is yet to come never falters. Well, maybe just a second or two, as he tells me his middle daughter has just been diagnosed with multiple sclerosis and can no longer walk.

But he recovers quickly and ends the grim announcement with, "Her mind is strong, and we're going to find a way to beat this thing. I'm sure of it." I believe my old friend.

We laugh, we reminisce, we exchange stories of our aging body parts and how it felt to receive our first social security check, and walk out to the parking lot. Bob points to a heap of scrap metal masquerading as a car, a multicolored, rusting, dilapidated old Chevy resting uneasily on four threadbare tires and laughs, "My car finally crapped out the other day, and my brother loaned me this survivor of the fifties. Hell, I may be living in it by Thursday."

More laughter as we both realize the irony of our dreaming.

"Isn't it something," he muses, as a light rain falls on the East San Fernando Valley.

"What's that, Bob?"

"Well, look at us. It's forty-five years later, and we're starting all over."

"I figure if George Burns could make a comeback at eighty, we're still way ahead of schedule."

Another punch line. More laughter, a long hug, and clenched fists against the heart. Bob starts up his wounded tank, belching thick black clouds of exhaust, and inches his way into the night.

I can hear his laughter a half block away.

MAN OVERBOARD

It was the silliest and most deadly whim I have ever entertained—to jump from the forecastle of the world's most luxurious cruise ship into the rich blue-black waters of the eastern Caribbean: to be engulfed by the darkness; to fight no force of nature, but to embrace it; to flow; to merely survive until first light the next morning; to watch the northern sky with a billion shimmering stars as my only preoccupation.

I stood at this railing, as I had every night since we sailed from Old San Juan Harbor, looking at the simplest of profound acts, a ship of the line cutting its way through the water, upsetting the rhythms of the ocean for just an instant as it maintains course and speed to a new port, a grand designer's perfect geometry. Clarity, purpose, logic, irrefutable basic magic, the pounding tattoo of water against steel, the occasional salt spray of a rogue wave defying the patterns of movement, climbing the weather decks washing away petty concerns. I was Ulysses, Sir Francis Drake, Columbus, Neptune, Prospero, pure spirit, free of my body, free to appreciate the only fact worth knowing—what a small part of the universe I was. This is the best moment of my life.

Why would I want to end it by hurling myself into 180 fathoms of treachery in the dead of night?

Was it a death wish? Was it the logical end for a hopeless romantic who had accomplished all his goals and needed one final flirtation with adventure? Maybe I wanted the clarity of my youth again; maybe I wanted the balm of simplicity poured over my media-bombarded senses; maybe I wanted my ears cleansed of modern tribal Rock and opened again to symphonies of summer memories; or maybe I just wanted an exclusive conversation with God. I don't know.

Whims have no reason, only muddled feelings propelled from an unknown place. Like an unforecasted tornado, they suddenly appear with overwhelming force, fully developed with a short but definite life of their own, seducing your imagination with one driving imperative, "Stop thinking. Just do it." A mystical fearlessness caresses the impulse, and there you are—bungee jumping over a swollen gorge or plummeting through clouds at the speed of an Indy 500 winner with your hand on a flimsy ripcord praying the huddled hunk of nylon on your back inflates before you join the road kill on Interstate 5.

We've all had this whim every time we look over the edge of a high place. It's in the "falling" dream we all share. It's in the deep down, dark place of our nature that operates independent of reason. It is that constant whisper that dares us to start all over.

I've heard the whisper five nights in a row, now I'm actually climbing the polished oak rails of the M/V Galaxy and leaping out into the cool tropical night.

My God, I'm doing it—and I'm smiling. I know I'm smiling. I can feel it in every part of my body. A wave-top spray washes across me like a giant baptism of welcome to a new world. Now I'm sinking below the surface, down and down. Put my arms out, relax. There, I'm heading upward. What's that?

Explosion, turbulence, ear drums vibrating—my God, the twin propellers of a seventy-eight thousand ton super liner making 27 knots is about to grind me into powdered fish food. You didn't jump far enough away from the ship. Don't open your eyes. Let it happen.

It doesn't.

I'm on the surface. I'm in the wake…lights from the ship strong enough for those passengers on the starboard side to see me. Should I shout and end this midsummer night's madness, or do I play out the string? Make up your mind, the ship is moving away fast. Oh, hell *Help, help, man overboard, over here, help, help*. They, ve gotta see me, I'm in the light. *Help, help*…pitch black darkness…stay calm, they heard you, the ship will start turning any minute. Remember your Coast Guard training; turn in the direction of the man overboard. They'll be turning hard to port any second. Water is warm, but a lot rougher than it looked from thirty feet above. No problem. Maintain your relative position. My God, what do I say when they pick me up? *Hey, it was just one of those primordial urges to take a swan dive into oblivion. No rhyme, no reason. Completely irrational, I admit it. Let's just forget the whole thing, okay? Drinks for the entire ship on me, okay?*

Sure, that'll draw rave reviews. Wait! The ship isn't turning. How could they have not heard me? Christ, I was two octaves higher than Pavarotti. Okay, okay, stay calm. You never planned on immediate rescue when you did the deed, remember?

Whatdahell did you plan on? Nothing. That's it, that's the point of this. No plan, nothing anticipated. Stick to your illogic. Don't do anything, just be. Wish I could get on my back and float. Never could float—how I tried as a kid. Swim, yes, simply roll over on my back, spread my arms and legs, and just let nature do all the work, no. Come on give it a shot. Whadahell else is there to do? Arms, legs out, head back, breathe normally, uh oh, keep the chest up. Hell, I'm doing everything right, and it's not working. Dammit, I can not float. Relax, try again. later. Slight current—point five knots, maybe—pushing me south out of the sea lanes. Not good. Better swim against it for awhile to compensate for the drift. Lights ahead—a ship—probably that Holland America liner that followed us out of the harbor. I can see both of her running lights Good, she's heading straight this way. Just over the horizon, twelve, thirteen miles away. Should be here in a half hour. I'll swim a little more against the current, rest, and drift back into the sea lane. Whew, tired already—a lot more resistance in the open sea than the ol' 40 meter pool at the Y. Rest, save your energy, look at those stars! Hey, big Dipper, howyadoin'? Down here, man overboard, longitude 65 degrees east, maybe 18 degrees north latitude. You look sensational, better than I've ever seen you. I know, I know, I look pathetic. You're right. I have no idea why I'm here. Ain't it great? I bet I'm the only fool in the water right now who can name all seven of your stars. Alkaid, Alioth, Megrez, Phecda, Merak, and Dubhe. Good ol' reliable Dubhe pointing the way to Polaris, the North Star. You probably saved more lives than all the medicine ever produced—the North Star and a little faith…what more do we need? Gotta go fellas. The ship is getting closer. Looks like it will pass close aboard—sure to be seen. In fifteen minutes I'll be drinking hot coffee from the captain's choice silver service and posing for the ship's newsletter with my smiling rescuers. The whole thing seems more Gilbert and Sullivan than an exercise in self-exploration. I feel different, so strange. I mean aside from the fact I'm fully clothed treading water in the middle of a great big ocean in the dead of night with a thousand things that can break the surface and take me to Hades in the flash of a single gulp. What is it?

I'm peaceful, that's it, above it all without fear. Why? Maybe it's time to stop talking, stop doing anything, and listen…just listen. Here comes the ship. Got to make sure I'm close enough to be seen and heard, but far enough away from their twin meat grinders. Got to swim against the current—good, good, I'm moving closer. It's just a few hundred yards away now. I should be fifty or sixty feet away from her starboard side. She's lit up like Times Square on New Year's Eve. Good. Plenty of light, no trouble seeing a waterlogged jerk in a green-and-yellow Hawaiian shirt ending some ridiculous rite of middle-age passage. Almost here. My God, am I too close, too far, what? No perspective, can't tell. I'm shaking; why not? Seventy thousand tons of steel bearing down on 185 pounds of flesh and bone. I can feel the vibration under water. There's the bow. Holland America Line…Rotterdam…famous old ship of yesteryear, when cruising was the exclusive domain of the landed gentry. Yes, there are passengers at the rail. Now, start yelling your brains out, wave your arms, take off your shirt and wave it now. What's wrong? Why aren't I yelling? Why? I can see their faces: the lady in a red dress; that man in a plaid jacket Shout, you fool, shout. There's that underwater explosion again, the twin screws are passing, so is your chance for being seen. People on the fantail…still time. Just open your mouth and scream. It's gone, the lights of Times Square are fading. What happened to me? I could have ended this thing, but I didn't. Do I really want to die or does this thing have a life of its own? Its own will, its own purpose, its own ending.

He drifted in silent disbelief for awhile, occasionally looking to the stars for answers. He tried and failed several more times to float on his back. He reached out a few times for what he thought was something drifting by, but soon found out every shadow looks like substance in the middle of a midnight ocean. His voice was weaker but calmer now.

He squinted at his watch.

What time is it? Hmmm, four hours to daybreak; four more hours with the equatorial current pushing me further and further south, away from land, away from the traffic latitudes into a thousand miles of uninterrupted ocean. I should be frightened, alert to possibilities, searching the area for some piece of flotsam, something to cling to, but I'm not. I'm just treading water in a slow, easy rhythm, and I'm okay…I'm okay. Maybe I shouldn't talk, conserve energy, shut down my motor, coast awhile, let the waves and the wind do all the work. Hell, no, that's suicide…gotta stay awake.

How long have I been in the water? What, two, no three, yeah, three hours, and I'm still here, still alive. That means something. That navigational light on the southwestern tip of Puerto Rico is barely visible. I'm drifting south faster than I thought…arms tired, time to float…yeah, easy for you to say…got to get on my back…come on. Whatdahell is so damn hard about learning how to float? Hey, hey, so far, so good, no, no, I'm falling beneath the surface. What is wrong with me?

I put two kids through college, made and lost two fortunes, survived a war, beat cancer and learned how to program that goddamn VCR, but I cannot float on my back! Why, God, why? What am I doing here? What new knowledge did I expect to find? Do I know anymore about myself, about anything than I did before? And why the hell am I not panicking? Because you don't care, that's why. I wonder what it feels like to drown…to slip below the surface of the world and become nothing. Will I black out before my lungs fill with salt water, or will I experience my death in each gasping moment? Will I know the very last moment of my life? Life is paradox—to have and to have not at the same time; to be in the midst of dying while still living; to be bored at the top of your game; to be bobbing up and down in the middle of a black ocean while singing the best of Sinatra, *"You'll never know just how much I miss you.*

You'll never know just how much I care…da da da da da dum da dum. Hmnnn, Hmnn, hmnn…October 8, 1957 a city died. Come on, you know what I'm talking about…that blackhearted son of satan, Walter J. O'Malley announced the Brooklyn Dodgers were moving to L.A. If you're at where I think I'm going, Walter, watch out. I'm coming for you and there's three million more of us who feel the same way. There's no hiding…if your soul is flying around up there, we'll find it you miserable traitor and tie it to a stake with Jeffrey Dalhmer's for all eternity…you broke my heart you Judas bastard. First base, Gil Hodges, second base, J-a-c-k-i-e, Jackie Robinson. Shortstop, Harold "Pee Wee" Reese, third base, Billy Cox. Left field, "Pistol Pete" Reiser. Center field, c-e-n-t-e-r-f-i-e-l-d, 'the Duke,' Erwin 'Duke' Snider. Okay, okay, Mays and Mantle had better numbers, I grant you, but to play with power and grace, in BROOKLYN, no less, come on, that's greatness. Right field, Carl 'The Reading Rifle' Furillo. On th mound, Preacher Roe, and behind the plate, Roy Campanella. Campy, God I miss Campy. I miss all you guys. You were the boys of summer, spring, fall and winter. You were the blue-collar heroes of my youth. You taught us all heartbreak is only a sometimes thing even for the underdogs…God, how I love that memory. Hell, life isn't paradox. Life is parody! Here I am ready to join the food chain for some Caribbean striped bass, and I'm doing an A & E Special on the Brooklyn Dodgers. I wonder what Jean Valjohn was thinking as he walked to the guillotine? Stars fading…waterproof watch stopped…close to sunrise…whadayaknow, I made it through the night, maybe…uh oh, here it is again, my old friend arthritis or is it bursitis, some damn "itis" in the right shoulder running all over my nerve endings. Can only tread water with one arm, now…not working too well…I'm okay…I'm okay.

He recreated all nine innings of a 1952 Dodgers-Cubs game, sang more songs, challenged God to a debate on genetic engineering, and had a lively talk with his dead father before his throat swelled from all the unintentional intake of salt water.

He became silent.

He continued to look for things, but wasn't too disappointed when he didn't find them. The lesson of indulging his whim was no clearer now than when he leaped from the deck of security into this dark, deadly uncertainty. His eyes moved from the clouds to the relentless cresting of the waves, and he accepted his insignificance, his total dependence on time and nature as only a man overboard can. He had no power to move anything but his own thinking.

The equatorial current carried him further and further south to a point where passing ships remained a tiny dot on the horizon.

He drifted four starry nights and three calm, clear days. The cracked lips, the sunburned skin, the nerve-damaged right arm dangling useless at his side made all movement painful, but it didn't seem to alter his thoughts. He continued to laugh a lot and loudest when he wondered why he had no expectation for the next moment. Soon everything left him, doubts, fear, faith and will. And, finally, he stopped thinking altogether, and that's when it happened. He was no longer an intruder, a stranger. He became part of all around him.

He was floating on his back.

THE RETURN OF
THE HUMAN FLY

Bailey Cobb and D.T. McCall were born just a few hours apart and less than a hundred yards from one another in the foothills of the Carolina Piedmonts.

For seventy-eight years they did everything together, farmed cotton, ran a gin mill, married the Burrey sisters on the same day, had three children apiece, joined the Army the day after Pearl Harbor, and became widowers shortly after their fiftieth wedding anniversaries. But for each similarity, there were a dozen darned good reasons why they shouldn't be great, devoted friends. Bailey was quiet, content with the moment, while D.T. was in perpetual motion, a searcher, a magician looking for a newer, more spectacular illusion to illuminate the day. Bailey accepted things; D.T. questioned everything.

"Hell, I don't understand why this town don't fight back. Look at all these stores boarded up. It's a damn shame," D.T. said, as he bit down on his peanut butter and banana sandwich.

"Everybody's going out to those malls, that's why," countered Bailey.

They'd had this same conversation every day for the last four years at about the same time in the same place—sitting on the rusting iron bench next to the twenty-seven foot high monument to the Confederate Dead. It would usually heat up about 12:15, with D.T. walking across the street to the steps of the century-old courthouse and shouting out to an unknown authority, "This town ought to fight back and keep these stores open."

Nobody paid much attention, after all, it was just those two good ol' boys from the John C. Calhoun Retirement Home for Assisted Living down the street. They were an accepted part of the fading landscape of North Main Street, downtown Anderson, South Carolina, a place where the word "emporium" still seems fitting for a large store. Everything was old in the "Electric City"—that's what they called Anderson, because it was the first town in the South to have an unlimited supply of hydro-electric power available for continuous use back in 1894. It was just a few years later that Oliver Bolt opened the first electric cotton gin in the world right there in Anderson, just a few feet from the Confederate Monument. Why this town actually was the second largest producer of cotton in the South at the turn of the century.

D.T. knew all this and was quick to stop folks on the street every chance he got and remind them of this proud heritage.

"Don't let this town die. Fight back. Keep the stores open. The hell with the malls," he'd say, and folks would do what they always did when the feisty old codger got up on his soapbox—they'd smile politely and walk on. Even Bailey would smile, even though he'd seen these kinds of outbursts ever since D.T. stood up in the middle of Easter services at the First Portman Shoals Baptist Church at three and a half and told minister Grady Isom, "You spit a lot when you talk."

Ninety-eight-year old Miss Addie Louise Perkins, formerly of Oconee County, now the caller at the nightly bingo games at the John C., would berate Bailey for putting up with his friend's "impolite ways."

His answer was always the same, "Miss Addie, being around D.T. is like hanging on to the tail of an ornery old bull. You just never know where you're goin' to end up, but it's always a heck of a ride."

By the time Bailey had finished his bacon and artichoke sandwich this day, D.T. had recalled every detail of Amelia Earhart's November 14, 1931 "drop in" with her auto-gyro airplane at the old Anderson airport, "Wasn't it amazin' how much Lindbergh and Amelia looked alike?"; watched him tell two bag ladies huddled around a shopping cart that "Melvin Purvis, the FBI guy that shot Dillinger, was from South Carolina, and so was Andy Jackson. I bet you didn't know that? "Then an animated lecture to unconcerned school kids" to remember that South Carolina was the first state to secede from the Union and become the center of the Southern Confederacy." As usual, Bailey smiled at it all.

A slight chill was blowing in from off Lake Hartwell. That was a sure cue for the friends to end the highlight of their day and start the three-block walk back to assisted living at the old John C. But first, there was one more ritual to perform. D.T. stood solemnly for a moment staring at the raised letters on the plinth between the first and second dies of the memorial base. Then with volume and grandilo-quent gestures that would have made the grand master of Southern oratory, John C. himself shake with pride, read the inscription, "To our Confederate dead…The world shall yet decide, in truths clear, far off light, that soldiers who wore the gray and died with Lee, were in the right." There was the customary pause followed by D.T.'s customary inquiry, "How'd I do this time, Bailey?"

Oh, about half a block, I'd say. You got as far as that policeman standing over there in front of Bryson's Cleaners giving us a dirty look."

"Hell, I must be losing it. Last week we got a rise out of those guys in suits outside Sullivan's Mortuary. That's got to be at least a full block."

They always walked a lot slower going back than coming. They knew what was waiting for them the rest of the day: idle chatter, lots of staring straight ahead in the day room, Parcheesi and whist tournaments in the game room, and, finally, more staring, this time at the two shiny paneled doors at the north end.

They swung open promptly at 5:15 PM every day heralding the last great anticipation in the lives of most of the 120 declining residents. Dinner, followed by more staring, an occasional coughing spree, and Mrs. Abilene Mae Boudreau's imitation of mild hysteria. She was convinced the black ladies on the serving line were poisoning her food to get back at her because her grand-daddy refused to free his slaves after the Civil War. No amount of assurance could dissuade her, so folks just went about eating their Apple Brown Betty and Pink Chiffon Pie and let her be.

Bailey took in all in stride for the price you had to pay for growing old on a modest pension. D.T. never would. He paused under the marquee of the ol' John C. once described as "the most elegantly appointed hotel south of the Mason-Dixon Line, a marble hall sanctuary, where nobility mixed with charm and grace produces the penultimate example of Southern Hospitality." Much of the restored charm remained in the gleaming Egyptian marble staircases, hand-crafted inlaid Florentine tile floors, and thirty-foot high cathedral ceilings with their solid mahogany beams and brilliantly colored dancing fleur-de-lis patterns. Built in 1925, the John C., at nine stories high, remained the tallest building in Anderson, a proud beacon of the best of yesterday for thirty-five years. But like all beacons, it finally burned out in the early sixties, when cotton and the thriving textile industry it spawned, sputtered and died. The John C. stood dark and empty for twenty years, entertaining little more than ghosts and tumbleweeds until revived into, as D.T. put it, "God's grand waiting room."

Bailey could see his friend was more reluctant than usual about entering the venerable old landmark.

"What is it, D.T.? Whatchagot in your craw?"

D.T. took a long look up one side of town and down the other before answering. "I spent my whole life within seven miles of this town, except for the war, and now, like me, it's old and dying, and nobody is doing anything about it."

Bailey hadn't seen his friend this serious since the day he got that visit from the Army man telling him his oldest son was killed in action in some village with a funny name in Vietnam.

"Well, D.T., there's not a whole lot two guys on Social Security can do about it. How about some pinochle?"

D.T. was thinking out loud. "Town needs a shot in the arm, something to get the blood moving again."

Bailey put a quarter in the newspaper machine and plucked out the last *Anderson* Daily Bulletin, *"Yeah, maybe we ought to bring back 'The Human Fly.'"*

"The Human Fly? Whatchatalkin' 'bout?" D.T. mumbled, still lost in thought.

"Don't you remember that daredevil fella back in '25 who climbed up the outside of the John C. the day it opened? Heck, must have been two, maybe three thousand people standing right here in the street watching the darn fool. Biggest thing ever to hit this town since the Yankees tried to catch ol' Jeff Davis running away with the Confederate treasury."

D.T.'s mind was racing far ahead of his words, "No, Bailey, I don't remember. Must have been the summer I spent with my mother's folks up in Spartanburg County."

A small but intense fire started burning inside D.T. McCall. It widened his eyes, quickened his steps, and overrode the throbbing arthritis in his knee joints, as he ran through the mummified starers in the day room and bounded up the main staircase to the mezzanine library. He pulled down the big black news-paper scrapbooks and quickly found the object of his search. As his index finger slowly moved over each word, he read aloud the June 22, 1925 headline and its accompanying story:

THE HUMAN FLY THRILLS THOUSANDS

As the largest crowd ever seen in Anderson County watched in stunned amazement, an unknown daredevil calling himself "The Human Fly," with the agility of a monkey in a tree, scaled the outside face of the newly opened John C. Calhoun Hotel on North Main and Orr Streets.

At 12 noon, he climbed up on the marquee and was already on the windowsill of the second floor when it happened. A great collective roar came from the frightened crowd, as the man slipped and fell backwards onto the roof of the marquee, one story below.

For a few seconds, not the least sound was heard, when suddenly, "The Fly" came to life, a slight trickle of blood was visible coming from a light cut over one eye. He very quickly resumed the climb and made it to the top amid the loudest boom of applause this town has ever heard.

D.T. bellowed the word "Yes" a dozen times, slammed shut the tired old scrap-book with such a thud, Mrs. Abilene Mae Boudreau began her catatonic fit two hours earlier than usual.

He spent the rest of the day calling area newspapers, radio, and TV stations alerting them that "The Human Fly" had returned and would be repeating his death-defying climb tomorrow at 12 noon, sharp. He likewise called three high schools, the Chamber of Commerce, the County Board of Supervisors, Hewlett's Dry Goods Store, and the local chapter of the Daughters of the Confederacy. At about 11:40 AM the next morning, the town of Anderson came to a complete halt. And that only happened twice before. Once on December 7, 1941 and way back on June 22, 1925. Aside from the noise of three fire engines, five sheriff's cars, two mobile TV trucks, and a helicopter from an Atlanta radio station, the scene around the ol' John C. was pretty much quiet. Even the evacuation of the residents was conducted in a relatively calm, orderly manner. For many of them it was the first time outdoors since their arrival, so naturally, they were more concerned with acclimating their eyes to the sun and staring at big modern machinery they had never seen so close up before.

D.T. and Bailey stood on the steps of Sullivan's Funeral Parlor across the street taking it all in.

"Whatdaya figure, bomb scare?" Bailey asked.

D.T. took a bite of his peanut butter and banana sandwich and replied matter-of-factly, "Nah, probably one of them damn civil defense drills."

As 12 noon approached, the crowd swelled so rapidly, all traffic in and out of town stopped in its tracks, occupants abandoned their vehicles and ran into the center of town. Bailey was so fascinated at the yellow-and-blue helicopter making loops and turns overhead, he didn't notice D.T. had quietly slipped away.

As the bells on top of the old courthouse finished their twelfth gong, an immediate silence came over the crowd. By now, they had all gotten word and were looking up at the John C. for the return of The Human Fly." Even the giant rotating blades of the helicopter seemed a lot quieter than just a few seconds before.

Nobody moved for a very long time until the word "hoax" started jumping from one group to another. Soon folks started breaking up and heading back to their routines.

Then it happened. Somebody shouted," Look, up there, on the marquee."

Sure enough, a man had climbed through a mezzanine window on to the roof of the marquee. He was wearing those old black-top sneakers everybody wore forty or fifty years ago, a baggy pair of work pants pulled tight with duct tape at both knees and ankles and a t-shirt with large handwritten letters on the front, "Fight Back!"

"My God, it's him, 'The Human Fly,'" shouted a voice from the crowd.

"Like hell it is," exclaimed an open-mouthed Bailey, "that's my damn fool friend, D.T. McCall."

D.T. waved grandly to the crowd below like one of those trapeze performers at the circus just before he shimmies up the rope to his swing. He then dramatically turned to the reddish-brown brick façade stretching nine stories above him and placed his foot in one of the creases separating the row of bricks. He pulled himself up to the next level. A giant wave of "ooohhs" and "ahhhs" rippled up and down North Main Street. Again, everybody froze. Even the police and firemen who were positioned to intercept the scheduled daring-do seemed hypnotized by this bold adventure.

"The Human Fly" had just passed the second floor window on a seemingly effortless pace upward to immortality when Bailey Cobb was heard to say, "Pretty damn good for a seventy-eight year old buck with no gall bladder, an artificial hip, and big black spots on his lungs."

As the big aerial ladder from the fire truck swung upward and was just about to move alongside "The Fly," reality overtook hope. The valiant climber lost his grip just below a fourth floor window and came sailing backwards into the warm Carolina afternoon. His arms and legs were spread wide apart, as if he wanted to feel the full joy of flight. Some folks disagree, but those who were close to the wall are certain the sound he made was much closer to a laugh than a scream.

The Return of the Human Fly occupied the front page of the local papers in four counties for thirteen straight days. Everyone had an opinion. One geriatric psychiatrist from Charleston said it was the result of "severe depression." A letter to the editor called D.T. McCall, "A heroic symbol of achievement for senior citizens everywhere. After all, he did get to the fourth floor."

Cars were now slowing down in reverence every time they passed the marquee. A rock climbing club up in Wheeling, West Virginia, was planning a group climb up the John C. on the anniversary of D.T.'s fatal attempt. Country and Western star, Johnny Cash, even flew into Anderson, spent two nights at the John C. and wrote "The Ballard of D.T. McCall," a real catchy tune that makes D.T. sound a lot like Davy Crockett.

Bailey Cobb sat on the old bench alongside the Memorial to the Confederate Dead and smiled at it all, then looked down at the yellow sheet of paper he found on his bed that day.

> Bailey, my old friend, I know you're thinking it was a damn foolish thing to do, but, whatdahell, it beats staring yourself to death. I'll see you soon."

D.T.

He read it a few more times and then walked across the street to the steps of the hundred year old courthouse and shouted out, "This town ought to fight back and keep these stores open."

WRITER'S BLOCK

(Unedited)
Saturday morning, December 1, 2001

It's eight o' clock in the morning, and I'm so damn bored with being bored that I'm unleashing the beast within…I don't give a damn…I'm sixty-five, too young to do nothing, too old to start all over again, and too smart to throw in the towel because the dream is over and there's nothing to replace it…I've always had a plan, a goal to the mountain-top and the passion to make it happen…Where the hell did it go? How can it stop without my approval? I can't believe my indeci-sion…Christ, I really don't know where to go or what world to con-quer anymore…Things that mattered once, don't now—how can that be? I'm an achiever, a class A persona with enough energy for three life-times…What the hell happened? I'm lying in bed with no deadlines, no projects, no will to do or be anything. The talent is still in place and very serviceable but, dammit, there's no passion, no juice fueling an idea, any idea…I've told my stories…I've put on paper everything I ever wanted to…The well is dry, for crissakes…For a guy who spent his whole life pretending he was a hero in the middle of a 1940 black-and-white B movie romance adventure, why can't I muster up enough pretend right now to take a meaningful step—write a poem, outline a play, devise a marketing strategy, reinvent myself, God, I hate that phrase…Something, what? I'll lie quiet, clear my mind, let the universe work within me...What kind of bullshit is that...I'm talking like a mindbender, for crissakes...Deepak, Tony, Wayne, Oprah and the other shit-shovelers making a pile of dough telling us all "how to" because we can't or won't take time to reason out the same line that's filling their bank accounts...Emerson was right, "...put no hope in the modern philosophers, they have no more connection to truth than you and I. They just spend more time thinking than the common man and arriving at the same conclusions available to all of us if only we would think."...Who am I bullshitting here? I was considered one of them myself. For years I traveled the country as a super motivator spewing my gems on 8x10 overhead transparencies and backing them up with funny anecdotes and lively group interactions that placed me at the top of the mindbender heap. Now, I don't give a damn...I want something more but I don't know what...Is that great irony or what, the teacher has run out of convictions...The Divine comedy is alive and thriving inside my empty brain...Let the beast roar...Do whatever you feel like doing at this moment, don't filter the urge through conscience, just fucking do it...Whatever comes knocking, just go with it...Why not, nothing else is working...Christ, I'm horny as hell...But you're always horny in the morning, most males are. It's the friendly wake up piss hard-on doing what it always does...The mating urge is roaring...Pick up the phone, call Christina...It's 8 o'clock in the fucking morning, for crissakes...What am I going to say, "Good morning, Christina. How's your day shaping up?? Want to fuck?"...Yeah, if that's the urge, do it...I'm dialing, it's ringing.

"Hello Christina, it's me. Did you ever wake up one morning and just decide to do whatever your urges tell you to do?"

"Yeah, I have, then I chicken out and go back into the same old routine of playing it safe. Doesn't everybody. Nobody gives a shit about what you really think or what you really need. They just want you to fit into their agenda, right?"

"Yeah, but that stops when you become 65."

"Why?"

"Because you suddenly realize your history is over, you don't fit in to anything anymore. You're angry as hell you're losing your greased lightning and the damned light at the end of the tunnel is getting bigger and bigger, so what the hell, if you wake up with a monumental erection one morning and feel it might be your last, you call a woman twenty-eight years your junior who thinks, to this point, you've just been a mentor and family confidante and tell her you want to make wild, passionate love to her all day, you do."

"You're writing a scene and need some realistic, gritty dialogue, right?"

"No, I'm not writing anything but checks these days. I've been diagnosed with terminal writer's block. Do you want to make love?"

Long pauses on the phone never portend glad tidings.

"I'm really freaked out...I mean super freaked. I've known you since I was a little girl...I mean, you were always a...."

"Father figure? Is that the phrase you're looking for?"

"I'm freaked. I have to hang up."

She does.

Swell, now she'll tell her mother, the wife of my ex-writing partner, who I was boffing for years while she was separated and a family friendship of thirty years is down the commode...You know what, I don't give a damn...I was only pretending to be a surrogate daddy all these years anyway...Who am I kidding, I did what I did so I could manipulate the kid into admiring my concern and care like the kindly old college professor who hopes the nineteen year old sophomore in the see-through blouse rewards his personal attention with a blow job...I'm tired of restraining my raging libido...Christ, I'm 65, what's the point in restraining anything...

Now what? Call someone else, ask for something, tell them off, tell them something I've always wanted to say but were too damn civilized to go from gut to mouth to their ears, what?

Ye shall know the truth and the truth shall make ye free...Bullshit! Lies make the whole damn thing work—marriage, relationships, history, religion, every freakin' conversation you'll have, all lies...Presentation, not substance...The truth is we're all pleasure seekers and we never get what we want when we want it and that's the underlying rub for everything we do twenty-four seven...What the hell is happening to me? Calling a young gal, blurting out I want to have sex with her, what the hell is that? Burnout, frustration, afraid of dying, what?...No, you're letting go of the façade, remember?...Bullshit, you're just bored to death because there's nothing left to do on your *To Do* list...You've done it all—paid all the bills, left some lightweight footprints in the sand and the world didn't quite recognize your genius as well as you do...That's really it, you want a bigger payoff and you're not going to get it...You're right back where you started...What the hell did I expect?...More, you expected more, and what the hell would you have done with more?...Chaplin was right...I hated the mean little bastard, never thought he was funny...But he got it right on his death bed..."In the end, it's all a joke."...Yeah, well that's no fucking consolation, Charlie, when nothing seems to matter anymore...I'll call Savanna.

"Dad, why are you calling me so early? Something wrong? What?"

"Well, aside from having evolved into a clinical state of 'I don't give a shit about anybody or anything,' and having no idea whatsoever what or where the brass ring is anymore, I'm fine."

"Whoa, this doesn't sound like you. What's going on? It's mom, she called you, right?"

"Your mother hasn't called me in twelve years. No. It's just December 1, D-Day for me. I don't know why, I'm just emptying out my storeroom of sixty-five years of stuff I never said or did. You won't understand it for another thirty years, but it'll happen to you. It's a major stop at the end of the line for all of us. It's like your soul just swallowed a gallon of Milk of Magnesia and the crap can't stop flowing. God, I'm such a romantic. The tank is bone dry and, maybe, that's a good thing. I don't know. The coroner hasn't arrived yet. Look, I called you because, hell, I felt like it. You and your sister have blamed me for the divorce all of your lives. Well, if I'm going to be the bad guy I want you to blame me for the truth, not the bullshit melodramatic garbage you've been handing me for years. I divorced your mother because I got sick and tired of living a lie, period. She's faultless, a living saint, we all know that. I married her without lust, only admiration. She was just too good, too special to let go, so I lied to myself and married her. But trading off sexual satisfaction to live with the most perfect human being I have ever known didn't work for me, so I pretended like every other guy in my generation—only they were better actors than me—they stayed faithful. I had affairs, lots of them but covered my tracks pretty good so you guys never knew."

"You're not only a bad actor, Dad, you're a lousy tracker, too. Mom knew.

We all knew, but nobody said anything. That's what the kids of my generation did. We saw things but we kept our mouths shut."

"Christ, all those years, all that lying, all that game-playing…"

"Yeah, but the leftovers were pretty good. We had a lot of love and laughs, and maybe that's the tradeoff mom accepted to keep us all going on the same track."

"Well, isn't that a kick in the head? I call to unload on you, and you turn around and unload on me."

"Haven't you learned by now all that lust crap is highly overrated? It's all temporary insanity. When it's over, what you're left with is what you're supposed to live with the rest of your life. And you and mom had a lot of great stuff still on the table. But, hey, what do I know? I don't have the advantage of testicles to guide my every thought."

"You should have been a writer."

"I am a writer, Dad, remember?"

"Advertising is not writing. It's prostitution with a lot of adjectives."

"Alright, let's not go down that alley again. So, when are you going to visit your grandchildren?"

"I don't like them. They're serial killers in training."

"They're only four and five years old, for God's sake. Grandpas don't have to like their grandchildren. They just have to show up from time to time."

"I'll call you again, soon. I've got another call coming in. Bye. (hangs up) Yeah, hello."

"For crissakes, Artie, Jean Marlton just gave me an earful. Said you called her daughter and wanted to get her in bed this morning. Did you OD on your Viagra or what?"

"I'm surrounded by hostile boredom, Jerry. Every damn way I turn I can feel my own inconsequence. Christ, I haven't done anything meaningful in the last six months since I bought a satellite dish. I've lost my juice, pal. I'm spending half my day trying to figure out what shows I'm going to watch on TV. I know the first names of every host on the goddamn Home Shopping Network. Whatdahell is that all about? I just can't make anything happen. It's like someone turned out all the lights all of a sudden."

"So propositioning young girls on the phone before breakfast is going to turn the lights back on? Whatdahell were you thinking?

"Excitement, hope, staying alive, I dunno. I wasn't thinking. That's the point. Christ, man, haven't you ever gotten to a place where you can't feel anything and you just have to do something to make sure you're still inside your own life?"

"Yeah, every time I go shopping with the old lady. You know what I think, pal? I think you're just like every other Gemini I know. You can't handle idleness. If you're not juggling four balls at once, you go nuts. You're a motion man, Artie, so get back in motion. If the writing thing has dried up, fuck it, do anything—volunteer at a soup kitchen, teach English as a second language, get some hair plugs, something."

"Thanks for the advice, Jerry. My universe is clear, now. Bye. (hangs up) Yeah, I'm a motion man, right…God I hate this…Nothing is preface anymore…And will you please stop complaining, that's not me…Dammit, I'm thinking, no good, no good…Back to the urge…Keep telling yourself all that we are and all that we can be is intuitive…Listen for the little voice…Let go, fuck it…Why the hell is every single urge about sex…Christ, I'm consumed by it…What is that? Is it sick, frustration, the morning hard-on, what?…No, sex is always there. It just takes over when you have nowhere else to go…So what's next?

On December 1,2001, Artie Werhaus, professional speaker and freelance writer, set a record in Boise, Idaho. He made 241 phone calls in a single day. He told the truth, whatever it was at that moment, shocking most and being shocked himself a few times.

He found out most people who knew him admired his talent and resilience to (here comes that phrase again) recreate himself every time life handed him a blow. His landlord lowered his rent a hundred dollars a month after being harangued for an hour with the argument that longtime loyalty deserved a discount.

He went a step further and persuaded the editor of the *Boise Register* to have him write a paid editorial advocating the city's Landlord-Tenants Association adopt a "Frequent Flyer" type program to reward long term renters with one month free rent every year. He convinced a former Army buddy he hadn't spoken to in forty-two years to bankroll a start-up porno website devoted to senior citizen's fantasies. And his ex wife explained in graphic detail why he was a lousy lover as a spouse before revealing she had carried on a torrid guilt-free affair with their parish priest most of their marriage. Fifteen women called him a dirty old man for propositioning them on the phone—two called the police and four invited him out for drinks. He felt exactly the same way when he woke up the next day, Sunday morning. He stared at the phone for a long time. Finally unplugged it and walked downtown where he volunteered as a food server at the Midnight Light Mission.

SITTING IN THE RAIN IN OLD HILO TOWN

Author's note: Hilo, on the Big Island of Hawaii, is yesterday, with its clapboard homes with tin roofs, wooden sidewalks, mom-and-pop stores with original paint jobs intact. It's old, rundown and proud. Except for the fact it is 2100 miles from California in the middle of the Pacific and fronts an idyllic half-moon bay, it could be any small town in America unwillingly fading into its own history.

I love to watch a town rise in the morning—the sights, the sounds, the unmistakable rhythms of birth are never quite the same but very close: the reluctant slogging to consciousness, as if sleep were the more natural state of being; the first smell, an amalgam of fresh-brewed coffee and the dew rising is the siren's call for all life to begin anew; yawning shop owners opening their doors, shielding their half-opened eyes from the early light; the first foot traffickers, the itinerants, the wanderers, the I-don't-give-a-damn crowd, a motley brotherhood of the displaced, crisscrossing the landscape without intent. Stop here, cross there, cross back, it doesn't matter, just move for movement's sake. Maybe mobility will bring purpose. Here come the empty school buses, yellow streaks darting to the outskirts like so many rattled birds shaken from hibernation, sad-faced drivers hunched over giant wheels, drowsy helmsmen anticipating another storm; clusters of strangers, heads bowed like philosophers in search of elusive syllogisms, standing at bus stops, tired yet anxiously waiting to be transported to places they don't really want to go.

Automobiles, just a few at first and then, suddenly, great numbers appear from all corners of the mist like self-propelled missiles in a bombardment frenzy. They bring a shrill, discordant ballet that delights no one but commands everyone's attention. The clarion call has sounded; the giant is stirring, the quiet is over—engines bark, voices shout, the ground rumbles, nothing is muffled, filtered or refined. Everything is raw, direct, as is. Every part of the whole vibrates to its own energy, nothing evolves, everything explodes.

Wonder and madness like colliding clouds melt into each other and become easy companions. Expressionless old men trapped in days that have too little of everything but time appear on park benches and watch the unsyncopated parade without comment, content to stare beyond it to some secret place known only to them. Soon nature's most assuring touch, sunrise, fades on the scale of importance as the city below trains its eyes on lesser things and roars to full power. A thousand disorganized movements of the same machine mysteriously blend creating order out of chaos. The unconducted symphony, the simple, confounding routine miracle of a new day is here.

THE HEROIC AGE COMES TO THE CHIRIQUI HIGHLANDS

It's strange what thoughts fill your brain when fatigue and pain are threatening to shut down your life force. He was at the end, no longer able to feel his large sinewy black arms cutting the still water. His six kicks per cycle were continuing to propel his slim frame forward under a starless night. He was conscious of motion, but from memory, not the moment.

Soon sleep would overtake his historic undertaking. His body would shut down, and he would be washed against the bulky silt of Barro Colorado Island or perhaps drift unnoticed alongside the railroad pilings, pulled north past Monkey Hill joining the other lifeless forms relentlessly being claimed by the Atlantic.

Then came the visitors, small pieces of the past, pictures, sounds, filling his consciousness. Making no sense. Pointing nowhere, just swirling about like the seedpods of the fallen cacao leaves dancing on the September winds in his father's orchards.

He thought, *Maybe this is what happens at the moment of death. With reason gone, the mind releases all its stored images and they simply float past the big screen inside your head one last time. A fleeting and final look before disappearing forever.*

They came in no particular order and, somehow, managed to keep his mind off the pain, while both arms and feet moving in the same synchronous rhythm kept him moving forward these past forty-one hours.

For a few seconds he was in the large irrigation ditch in the sugar cane fields of the Chiriqui Highlands outdistancing the other boys, smiling, stroking evenly, feeling free of the endless routine of field work. Another second he was carrying the battered old wicker basket filled with his father's lunch: black beans, maize, a soft ripe coconut, and a tin of ponga juice, a staple of his West Indies heritage, carefully prepared by his mother every day. A half dozen different citrus fruits smashed into pulp and floated in a generous portion of rum. Next came the earth-pounding sounds of the giant 95-ton Bucyrus steam shovels with the claws of a prehistoric monster digging deep into the mud of Culebra and depositing two tons of the dark slimy gook into the large "earth trucks" with tires as big as any building in his mountain village. Rattling locomotives, grinding concrete mixers, squealing cables and the thunder of crushed rock being dumped. He heard it all just as he did ten years before standing amid the 40,000 other ants dwarfed by the giant machinery eating along the Continental Divide through fifty-six miles of solid rock mountain and impenetrable jungle to construct the impossible.

"Poppi, Poppi, is that you?" he muttered. "Look at me, Poppi, look at what I'm doing."

Suddenly, the burning pain in his lungs was gone. So, too, were the stabbing knife points jabbing his back and shoulders with every stroke.

It was his father, proud, seemingly undaunted by the oppressive 130-degree jungle heat, loading large, jagged chunks of the shiny, red igneous rocks into the big iron bin suspended from the crane a hundred feet above. He could see it, more clearly than the freshly painted red and green channel markers just a few feet either side of him, more real than the dark brooding waters all around him.

It was midnight in the horse latitudes on a moonless night, but Balboa de Lesseps Ycaza, son of outcast peasant parents from the lesser Antilles, farmer, dreamer, the best mountain ditch swimmer in the entire country, could clearly see and hear them all.

Delusions, phantasms, or perhaps whispers from friendly spirits gifting him with the only antidote available for his pain. It didn't matter. The pictures fed his motion forward, ever forward toward his rendezvous with history or oblivion.

Small pieces of flotsam, tree branches, wooden boxes, metal banding driven down the rain-soaked hillsides of the nearby Chagres River were forming an unavoidable mine field all around him. He didn't see them. He didn't feel their sharp edges ramming his body in a dozen places, opening the skin, tearing apart what was left of his skin-tight black cholo shirt. Now, his patched brown short pants would be his only protection against the elements.

He lifted his head a few inches higher out of the water in search of La Sugre, a rare cooling August breeze that mysteriously sweeps down from the north around Galeta Island and delivers a momentary reprieve from the stifling heat and humidity of the devil's breath. The local San Blas Indians believe it is the harbinger of the dreaded monsoons. If he could find it, maybe the cooler air would soothe his swollen nostrils and, at the same time, confirm he was still swimming in straight lines, on course to the prize. He took a deep breath and filled his lungs. No relief. It was the same smothering hot, rancid air he had been breathing at every stroke of the journey since sneaking down the hillside and entering the water at Quarry Heights on the Pacific side a day and a half ago.

"Dear Jesus Christus," he mumbled. "If you choose not to help me, then please don't work against me. Open the clouds, let the moon shine, give me light. Let me find my way."

Like every other prayer he'd ever offered, this one, too, went unanswered.

He went back inside looking at more pictures. A broad grin suddenly started in the corner of his swollen lips and erupted into a full smile, cracking the sun-burned blisters ringing his sunken cheeks. It was an old smile, the kind he always wore when his father beckoned him from the bottom of the muddy hell below, the signal it was all right for him to descend the dangerous, slippery embankment into the world's largest and most famous ditch. His slender ebony frame negotiated the heavily creviced rock-embedded wall like a cheetah in full stride. He knew this land. He was part of it. It could not hurt him. He felt the admiring eyes of the hundreds of sweat-soaked workers in his father's section watching his balletic sprint to the bottom of the pit. He could feel his feet sink into the primordial ooze all around him, as his father took the basket from him and offered to share half his lunch. Ah, such a moment. No other twelve year old boy in the universe could claim it. It was all his. Seven days a week, fifty two weeks a year. Surrounded by heroes pulling, loading, digging, blasting, pushing back the mountains and jungle, rearranging the geography of time. They came from faraway places he could never imagine. He could see their leathery, weather-beaten faces, burned, scarred, enameled in the colors of the earth around them, the brotherhood of laborers forever destined to slog from one project to another to make the dreams of other men come true. Whites from the Po Valley in Italy; North Americans from the Yukon Territory to the mountains of Appalachia; Russians, Germans, Poles, and 30,000 blacks like himself, descendants of freed slaves throughout the Caribbean. They would die, black and white, by the thousands in mudslides, avalanches, flash floods, fever and sheer exhaustion, but they were part of something so much bigger than themselves that a hundred generations from now their common indistinguishable faces would still be young, frozen in this time in a thousand historical photographs validating they were here. They alone made the miracle happen.

The evolution of mankind toward a higher destiny was at work in this godforsaken isthmus of tormenting heat, disease, and historical despair. The heroic age was being born. Insignificant men leading insignificant lives were now risking all to be a part of it. Young Ycaza desparately wanted to be counted among them.

"Poppi, when can I work here with you? I am strong. I'm ready."

"You are destined for greater things than this, my son. Doesn't your name tell you that?They will sing the praises of your victories at the Santo Cristobal festival for as long as the corn grows high. Be patient. This is not your time, but soon. Soon." His father smiled and rubbed the back of his son's neck. Young Ycaza knew this was as close to a hug as a proud man gives, but it was good enough.

He could feel it now. He felt it everyday of his life since that last day in the pit.

The next morning his father's name appeared on the white paper tacked under the heading "Today's Notices" on the paymaster's shack.

Emanuel Galos Ycaza, tag No. 437692, was crushed
to death in the pulleys of a mud scow yesterday

He carried that piece of paper neatly folded in the watertight sheep-skin bag tied to his belt along with sticks of beef jerky, coconut slices and the tin of fresh water.

He was on his own now in the pitch blackness, unaided by any navigational fixes other than his instincts. He just couldn't think about it.

He retreated back to the pictures in his mind.

There he was walking along the row of tree-shaded white houses spraying oil on still water, a metal tank on his back. White ladies in elegant summer dresses behind the neatly screened enclosed porches served afternoon tea and paid no attention to him or the hundreds of other black workers ridding the land of the deadly Anopheles mosquito.

Often they would yell, "Boy come in here. I see one. Come quick."

He would. Along with his chloroform and glass vial he would painstakingly catch the deadly insect and rush it to the hospital laboratory on Ancon Hill for analysis.

Was not this a significant achievement worthy of recognition during Santo Cristobal days? Was he not part of the greatest medical victory of the young twentieth century, the eradication of Yellow Fever in the tropics? Surely this would be recognized. It was, but like his father and the other men who pushed back the wilderness in the pit, they would be relegated to group pictures of scruffy men in dirty overalls standing at the bottom of the largest manmade hole in the world. Afterthoughts to brighter lights above. Only the men in white suits and straw hats sitting behind big desks would have songs written about them, shake hands with presidents and kings and have their names inscribed on shiny iron plaques in the parks.

Great times are no different than bad ones. They cast giant shadows of shame. The strict caste system imposed by the men in white suits left him very few options for a life of distinction: porter, janitor, garbage man, gravedigger, or mud hog in the pit. He would have to find a another way to overcome the sociology of the times and fulfill the promise of his name.

Suddenly the pictures were gone.

He had run into an obstacle that demanded attention.

"What's this?" he muttered. Slowly he felt the spongy mud around him.

"Wait a minute. I can stand." A small opening in the clouds lasted long enough to reveal the most welcome surprise in forty-eight hours of swimming, floating, avoiding detection.

"Yes, it's the finger islands. Must be. But which one? Look for the lights, Balboa, remember to look for the lights."

He drew himself up on solid land. He couldn't feel his body, but a renewed burst of energy had his tall, willowy frame standing, searching all points of the compass for signs.

"What's that, in the distance? Yes, a light, one, two, three, four…every four seconds. The navigation light at the foot of Fort Randolph. Yes."

He had read about it in the Zone Gazette.

> *A brand new aide to navigation, an occulting electric light housed in a double-glass spiral casing was placed on the rocks below Mount Hope today. It is set intermittently to shine for two seconds and be off for four. This will identify the rugged shallow marshlands and warn local mariners of danger. It will also serve as a fixed bearing.*

He extended his right arm in the direction of the light and held it firm, as he scanned the darkness in slow movement searching for another sign.

"Is that a…yes, it is, one, two three lights. What, maybe 45 degrees off the horizon."

He extended his left arm in the direction of the new lights and looked at the angle made between his arms.

"Must be the parapet lights of Fort Davis at the southern tip of Limon Bay."

His shout pierced the black night and reverberated through the still jungle underbrush like a thunderclap in a box canyon.

"Thank you, Jesus Christus. T-h-a-n-k Y-o-u!"

He sat on the rocky shore, smiling, repeating the same name over and over.

"Isla Major. Isla Major."

For once, fortune had been kind and carried him through the impenetrable darkness to this shore. It was beyond reason and mere mortal strength. A myth was being born.

He had entered the Pacific, navigated through fifty-two miles of two bays, the treacherous serpentine Gaillard Cut with no straight lines, only twists and turns that would exhaust any living creature. He swam against the tide of the mighty Chagres. Entered the 163-square mile labyrinth of Gatun, the largest manmade lake ever constructed, with a hundred deceptions to victimize all but the chart makers. He had done all this on a steeled determination aided by pictures of the past, instinct and the sound of his father's voice. "You are destined for greater things…" He was less than a mile from the starting point of the final leg of his incredible journey. Unconsciously he reached into his sheepskin bag and removed half a coconut shell. He had earned a reward. It never made it to his lips. Sleep was instantaneous.

On August 15,1914, the sun rose slowly over the Andes. Half the population of the tropics was already hard at work, tilling, planting, cutting, hauling, sweating in the sucking humidity of another equatorial summer, buying another day of survival in a land notoriously unconcerned for human dreaming. Life, death, poverty, night, day were all the same, tediously woven into one large ragged mosaic constantly unraveling at the edges.

Any slight glimmer of hope always seemed to be overshadowed by titanic events sweeping down from elsewhere, but rarely effecting the daily life of these people.

The storm that had been gathering in Europe since June had exploded just a few days before. The world was marching toward war. Page two of the newspapers was occupied with men in white suits gathering in San Francisco to decide if the largest exposition in the universe would go forward as planned.

The monumental achievement down here that was about to change the commerce of the world forever slid unnoticed into the back pages.

No world luminaries were on hand. No smartly attired military bands heralding the attention of the gods. No fancy ladies in lace parasols sitting royally in fine carriages or newsmen lugging large boxed cameras into position to record the miracle, just the constant drone of a few dozen excited rag tail workers in coveralls and heavy shoes milling around not knowing what emotion to express. An outsider coming upon the scene might think it was just another day at the worksite, routine, business as usual. It wasn't. It was the opening chapter of the most gilded, preposterously unimaginable and, ultimately, the most terrifying century of all time, the heroic age.

All eyes were on the stern-faced old man in the white suit and large straw hat cautiously checking the railroad tracks aside the giant cement locks of Gatun. George Washington Goethels, stoic, with the quiet arrogance of a Roman general surveying a battlefield, was the unquestioned ruler in this land. An acknowledged living deity by virtue of genius not title. All would take their cue from "The Solomon of the Isthmus," a man who proved the impossible is nothing more than a lack of determination to find the right mathematical equation.

He raised his right arm slowly, and the Ancon, an undistinguished small concrete-carrying freighter lying to outside the breakwater, headed for the channel center line and entered Limon Bay steady on course to write her name in the history books.

All eyes were seaward.

No one saw the smooth, even thirty-two strokes per minute of the black man cutting through the water far behind them.

If his luck held, he would arrive at the southern end of the locks about the same time the Ancon arrived at the first northern lock three thousand feet ahead.

The convergence of two historic events often cause great irony for one of them.

Amazingly, the opening of the Panama Canal drew little attention around the world.

It belonged to a yesterday that was fading quickly under the guns of August.

All eyes remained elsewhere.

The headline in the Canal Zone Gazette was the exception:

"The Greatest Engineering Work of All Time Opens For Business!"

On the back page, squeezed amid large ads for kerosene lamps, tonic water and a new popular cure-all, Haywood's Rectal Ointment, was a column of afterthoughts, titled, "Bits and Pieces." The detritus of the day, short articles about segregated schools working well for both blacks and whites; an excerpt from True Crime Magazine naming Mamie Lee Kelly, brothel owner of the Navajo on I Street, as the most notorious madam in the world and one more:

> Opening day of the Canal was not without a laugh. A black West Indian man was spotted swimming inside the Gatun Locks just as the Ancon entered on her historic voyage. To the cheers of the assembled workers, he finished his lock swim, climbed out at the northern end and declared his name was Balboa de Lesseps Ycaza. He made the wildly absurd claim he had just swum the entire length of the canal, fifty-six miles, with one six hour rest stop on Isla Major. More laughter, of course. Canal police were desposed to look the other way on this harmless fraud. Obviously, the chap had dropped into the final lock just as the front gate was opening in hopes of creating some attention. He handed an unamused George Goethels a small sheet of paper from a sheepskin bag attached to his waist and disappeared into the jungle.

On June 28, 1923, Richard Halliburton, bon vivant world traveler, and best-selling author, gained world headlines by becoming the first man to swim the entire length of the Panama Canal. He did it in installments one day at a time over a seven-day period, and was attended by a small entourage of yachts that included politicians, movie stars, bootleggers, a medical team, his personal chef and the president of the National Geographic Society.

The event drew no attention in the lush green fields of the Chiriqui Highlands, where the annual rich harvests of sugar cane, mangoes, bananas, and cacao are celebrated in the week-long festival of Santo Cristobal. They eat, they dance, they parade through a dozen local villages and sing songs of one of their own, an irrigation ditch swimmer and dreamer with a heroic name.

WAITING FOR
MORRY

Sunday, January 5, 10:27AM.

Waiting for Morry. He has two tickets for the Clippers basketball game this afternoon, and his wife doesn't want to go.

"Christ, I do everything for that woman. Go where she wants to go when she wants to go. Eat her damn vegetarian meals. Build her a damn indoor hydroponics garden, so we can eat more of that crap, and I get two courtside seats for a game, and she says she's got 'female problems' and she has to stay home. Every time I ask her to do something I enjoy, it's the same damn thing. 'I've got female problems.' Hell, you never hear men say, 'I'm sorry honey, I can't go shopping with you today, I've got male problems.' Where's the compromise? Where's the partner-ship? We probably should have had kids; then she wouldn't have time to have female problems. So, you wanna go, pal? I'll pick you up at 11:30 sharp. Okay?" I said, "Sure."

I don't know why. I don't like the Clippers, and I haven't attended a matinee of anything since watching Rod Cameron as Rex, the G-Man, every Saturday at the Acme Theatre in 1947. Nine year olds don't think about it, but self-medicating old men with unpredictable bladders instinctively understand there's just something unnatural about attending any indoor event in the middle of the afternoon.

I said yes, so I'm waiting. Maybe it's because I'm a Gemini and I just can't say "no" to any invitation. Maybe it's because we go way back together when we both had a plan to the top of the mountain, and I sense he wants to talk about old-guy issues. Why do I see the onset of *rigor mortis* when I look in the mirror but still feel seventeen on the inside; or is it me or is time moving faster when you're over sixty; and what happened to our dreams; and why don't we give a damn about anything anymore? It's the same old litany of male reckoning with mortality that routinely arrives with the first sighting of liver spots.

Probably that, but who knows? So, I'm waiting.

Funny the things you do while you're waiting for someone. I got up at seven o'clock and started cleaning the house. Why? I've never let him inside before; always came up with an excuse to avoid it. The painters are redoing my walls; the landlord's inside doing his annual inspection; I'm doing my taxes and they're all over the floor; no place to walk. That kind of harmless deflection. It's not that I'm a slob. It's just I've got this thing about privacy. Like all bachelors, my apartment is my haven for unguarded self-indulgences and I don't share that side of me with anybody but the gas man. I guess it's a Gemini thing. Who knows?

Makes no sense. He's not coming in anyway. Said he'd honk, and I'd come out to meet him. Nevertheless, here I am with my rubber gloves, Old Dutch Cleanser, and knee pads.

Well, you never know. He might have to take a leak and need to use my bathroom. God forbid he should see how I really live. Everything in piles, neat, mind you, but not the kind of décor a guy who color coordinates his underwear with his socks would approve. Not that I need or seek other's approval. Never have. Never will. Okay. Windows cleaned, toilet scrubbed, three weeks of cheese and macaroni remains scraped from the microwave. Wait a minute. What's the matter with me? Who the hell comes into your house and goes straight to the microwave for a white glove inspection? What's the point? And why the hell am I making the bed? Just close the door.

Because my mother is looking down from the family photo. "Half clean is not clean." That's why.

I'm not complaining. I like housework. Instant gratification. Immediate sense of achievement. If the day doesn't hold small victories for me, I'm dead in the water. No rudder control. No motion forward. No meaning. Cleaning-the-house therapy has done more for neurotics, insomniacs, and Geminis than all the shrinks and "How to" books combined. Forget the psycho-babble. People need results to drive away the blues. Thank God for housework. Dusting, polishing, stacking neatly, sticking unfinished projects under the bed, a touch of Tropic Tradewind air freshener aerosol spray in all rooms and, maybe, vacuum the rug.

No, it's fine. Besides, I'm tired.

10:31 AM. What now? An hour to kill. God, I hate that expression. I read somewhere the average adult wastes 4.1 years of his life just waiting—waiting on lines, waiting for other people; just nothing. Waiting for the next inconsequential consequence to show up, like old guys sitting on a park bench.

I'll read *Short Cuts*, an anthology of Raymond Carver's critically acclaimed short stories about...here we go again—nothing, simple, mundane moments in the boring lives of the unnoticed. The introduction says, "Carver is a master of American fiction, making poetry out of the prosaic." Is it me? Divine intervention wouldn't make this drivel poetic. Two guys eating cheeseburgers and drinking coffee at a hash joint looking at the waitresses' behinds; a middle-aged married couple house-sitting for neighbors debating whether or not to take a peek in their drawers; a baker who was glad he wasn't a florist, because baking is a better smell than flowers. What's the point? That's it. There is no point is the point. Christ. Ever since Beckett's *Waiting For Godot*, writers have been obsessed making nothing look like something. No beginning, middle and ending, just tiny random acts leading nowhere. Is that what modern storytelling has become? Unconstructed ennui. The hidden life of the avocado has replaced London's "White Silence," Poe's "The Cask of Amontillado" and "Saroyan's Resurrection of Life"—titans of meaning, stories that transported you above the sadness of petty routine. Farewell to romance and adventure. Hello waitresses' asses and neighbor's drawers. God, I hate losing my history. I wouldn't be caught dead writing a short story about nothing. I mean, what's the point?

I think I'll vacuum the rug.

11:30 AM. Morry's honking. My God, what is he driving?

"Hey, hey Morry. What the hell is this? A yellow submarine on wheels?"

"The Ferrari F 355 convertible, 3.5 liter, 375 hp, V-8. Top speed, 177mph. Runs 0-60 in 4.6 seconds. The Babe pick-up factor is off the charts. Christ, I have little old ladies in walkers waving at me. You like?"

"I like. Geez, I can't believe your wife would go along with this."

"She doesn't know. It's a lease. I keep it in a friend's garage for special occasions. Hey, I've really got to go. Mind if use your apartment to take a leak?"

"Sure. It's a mess, but go ahead. I'll wait."

SOME MEN LIVE BY BREAD ALONE

Jake "The Great" Boerket was the life of the party, and Seattle was his adoring host for twenty-five colorful years. At eighteen minutes after 5:00 and 10:00 PM Monday through Friday, 62.1 percent of all residents from Snohomish to Centralia were clicking to KING-TV, Channel 5, to see what the world's most entertaining weatherman was up to. Would he be challenging a Chicano gang in a dark alley in the seedy Pike section of the waterfront? Narrating his own open heart surgery?

Or maybe dangling by a rope on the Space Needle six hundred five feet above the Seattle Fairgrounds on his way to either a messy ending or a new entry into the Guinness Book of World Records?

Jake's three-and-a-half minutes of cold fronts, barometric highs, and five-day forecasts were always secondary to where he was and what he was doing. Stay tuned for the ten o'clock news. See Jake "The Great" live on the slopes of an erupting Mount Pinatubo or inside an Air Force WC-130 weather plane flying into the eye of an oncoming hurricane or anywhere else the big story was unfolding.

It was old-time television with hokey old-time hype, but somehow Jake's anachronistic persona hung on. Maybe television did have a heart after all and just couldn't let go of it's last cowboy, or maybe the sales department figured as long as Findler Motors was willing to pay two-and-a-half times the going rate to sponsor Jake's shenanigans, it could ignore the pressure from the home office to replace him with one of the younger, pretty people.

Jake never thought about these things. All human behavior was eventually absurd to him. Besides, the world always needed another clown, so if his time came he would just automatically appear in another circus down the road. He was the rarest of all modern animals, content, happy in the moment. He had a two-story custom made houseboat in the trendy Lake Union area, a twenty-foot Winnebago, a 1929 four-door Model A Ford in mint condition, a ranch in Jackson Hole, and the world's largest collection of the letters of P.T.Barnum. But it was the work, always the work, that fired his passion and pushed his spontaneity to exceptional places ordinary men could only imagine. He had, of course, paid a price for that choice—no wife, no children, no familial ties that bind. Jake always thought that was a fair trade-off for his all or nothing commitment to keep the word "great" between his first and last name.

The pre-dawn full moon over the southeastern corner of the Diamond Head crater was still high in the black pearl Hawaiian sky as Jake arrived at the front gate to the Punchbowl Cemetery, the final resting place for those Americans killed in the Pacific War. He flashed his press card to the starched and shiny Marine sentry.

"Kind of early, sir. The ceremonies don't start for three hours, and the gate doesn't open for another," he raised his left arm in that precise snappy way men assigned to VIP sentry duty are trained to do, quickly read the luminous dials of his government-issued black watch with the khaki wristband, and continued, "twenty-seven-and-a-half minutes."

"I know. I just wanted to secure a choice position for my camera-man to cover the President's speech before the mob arrives," he smilingly shot back.

The young Marine was getting ready to recite his standing orders, when a tall man in a dark gray suit and tinted blue glasses shouted from behind a parked limousine a few feet away, "My God, Jake 'The Great' Boerket. I might have known you'd be the first one here."

It was Al Stevanski, the President's advance man and former editor of the *Seattle Times*. They shook hands vigorously, and Al instructed the sentry to let Jake in. He did.

Jake lied. His cameraman was sound asleep on a 747 halfway across the Pacific heading home with twelve hours of Jake's coverage of the four-day commemoration of the fiftieth anniversary of V-J Day, the end of World War II in the Pacific. It was America's final observance of an incredible era, the last hurrah of a fading generation saying amen and walking away from the ghosts of Pearl Harbor, Hiroshima, and all the other bloody places between.

This morning's service would be the crowning event, attended by the President, Bob Hope, the surviving Andrews Sisters, brass bands, a small contingent of Japanese veterans carrying a large, gold friendship plaque and three thousand old men in Aloha shirts, polyester pants, pot bellies and chests full of multicolored combat ribbons. Yesterday on the deck of an aircraft carrier moored alongside the Arizona Memorial, the President called them, "...the boys who saved the world when it faced its darkest hour."

It seemed Jake had talked to them all. Long after the camera stopped rolling he sought them out, sometimes just to be in their company to listen to their playful, guileless chatter, to feel their hearty simplicity, and to remember another time when reality though harsh was unmistakably clear, goals were shared, and the community understood the pursuit of selfless higher purpose. These were uncustomary nostalgic pauses Jake had never taken, and he didn't understand why he was doing it now. Hell, he was only a kid during WW II, and not very interested at that. Sure he joined the newspaper and scrap metal drives and emptied his pockets of spare change during the War Bond appeals at the Belvedere movie Theatre, but that was only because his last name was Boerketstrasser and he didn't want the other kids to think he was a Nazi spy. "Patriotism" was just another tough word on the spelling test for young Jake. He was more interested in producing a junior USO Show for his neighbors in his backyard, where the proceeds from the customary collection by-passed the war effort and went directly to the White Owl cigar box under his bed. The most devastating war in history was simply a big break for a young entertainer who saw no real meaning beyond the footlights.

Jake "The Great" was the model Plato had in mind when he defined successful existence as one lived as if it were play.

Until now.

Something was changing, and Jake wasn't sure it was from within or without. He didn't even know why he woke up at 4:00 in the morning and felt compelled to be in this place at this moment.

He stood alone among 35,000 simple gray headstones as an early morning mist sweeping down from the Koolau Mountain range joined the first shards of daylight piercing the holy stillness of this magnificent outdoor cathedral. A solemn silent narration was everywhere. It spoke of heroism, sacrifice, and lost youth. It spoke of many other things once common to a nation in peril, things now fading along with the generation represented in this hallowed ground. Jake listened to it all, perhaps for the first time. He leaned against the giant jacaranda tree spreading shade over a dozen graves and didn't move through four hours of speeches, a missing man flyover by roaring Navy jet fighters, prayers, hymns, a twenty-one gun salute and a haunting rendition of taps that seemed to hang in the air long after the thousands emptied the historic crater and boarded buses back to the rest of their lives.

The cool mist gave way to a burning sun, which in turn gave way to dark clusters of colliding cumulus clouds, and then back to mist. Time evaporated, and Jake stood motionless lost in a strange state of nothingness. No thoughts, no purpose, no form. Nothing. Just a consciousness pushed beyond the moment to a quiet place he had never been.

"It's one of the great things that can happen to a man, to be here, to come back." Jake hadn't noticed the old man in the wrinkled blue-and-white Veteran of Foreign Wars cap leaning against the other side of the tree, but he responded casually as if they were familiar partners in this silent vigil, "Why is that?"

The old man shifted his weight from one leg to another the way old men do when standing is a painful necessity. The medals on his barrel chest jingled, and the tarnished gold one attached to the blue ribbon around his neck caught the light and sent a quick flash into the gray drizzle and just as quickly disappeared.

"Because there's no doubt here. Just," he hesitated to listen to the words forming inside and continued, "just meaning. It's good to know you were part of something greater than yourself...that for a few short terrifying moments your time mattered. Know what I mean.?"

He didn't wait for a response, and Jake didn't have one anyway. The old veteran smiled, looked up in the gray metal overcast trying to retrieve some part of yesterday, but it wasn't there. He held his hand out to catch some raindrops and quietly spoke the words that hung everywhere in the air for these last three days of final tribute, "Well, the chapter is over. Now I guess we all just fade into history."

Jake and the old war hero stood there in the rain under the big tree for a very long time like children on the last day of summer, reluctant to begin a new season. Finally, the old man walked slowly toward the main entrance and disappeared among the golden plumeria and scarlet anthuriums ringing the outer walls.

Jake never forgot that slow walk. It popped into his consciousness at the oddest moments of his life. It was there six weeks later when Findler Motors dropped their sponsorship of the weather show and Jake was replaced by one of the pretty people. And it was there every time he went looking for another circus down the road and couldn't find one.

THE LADY ON THE
PLANE

I always put myself in a mellow frame of mind for airline flights.

I'm reading the essays and criticisms of John Updike, she's playing electronic poker on her pocket-size game boy. I'm relishing delicious metaphors like "electroencephalograms of dreamers to endocrinial casts of fossil skulls," while she stares blankly like a mutant subspecies at tiny digital hearts and clubs on a thimble size screen, occasionally pressing buttons, winning and losing without a hint of emotional involvement.

I'm floating effortlessly with the Muse, being lulled like a full moon seen from a deserted tropical shore. She's squirming in her seat tugging at her underwear through her cotton-blend purple-and-orange jogging pants. I'm mellow, content to separate from the forced banter of strangers on a plane. She's restless, searching for contact. Later, I'm *Entrepreneur* and *Fortune* magazines; she's *Hollywood Gossip* and the expanded anniversary edition of *People* magazine. I highlight and take notes; she fast forwards through the pictures mumbling a running fashion commentary like, "Magenta earrings, cool" and "Birkenstocks with socks, tacky". My typical male kidneys are enormous bottomless tanks storing vast amount of liquid, while I remain biologically quiet and sedentary. She sips and runs to the john six times. I'm occupied with ideas; she's looking for things. I'm fascinated with my moments; she's terminally bored.

Amazing how our democracy still flourishes, when so many of us have so little intellectual currency in common anymore.

Long flight. Arrive early. A relief. Uh, oh, our gate isn't ready, so we have to wait on the tarmac. No problem, got plenty of time for my connecting flight. I'll go over my notes. She's sleeping. Half-hour, still waiting. Air conditioning malfunctioning.

Another ten minutes, still waiting. Getting antsy. Hell, my under-wear is sticking. Okay, I've read my notes, finished three magazines. Maybe back to Updike. God, it's stifling in here. Can you believe this guy makes a million a year sitting in his preppy sweater in the high-rent district of Connecticut writing stupid metaphors like this: "His speculation that the rounded breasts of the human female are imi-tations of the buttocks evolved to reinforce frontal sexuality in our uniquely upright social species of primate was as trivial as the hissing of a non-venomous snake." What crap. Okay, that's it. You want to win every major award there is in modern literature—simple. Become a metaphor junkie, for crissakes. Learn to compare big tits with a snake hissing, and the Pulitzer is yours, pal.

Ten more minutes.

What now? Gotta go. Still holding on the damn tarmac. Got the sweats, restless. Christ, there's no air in here. Why the hell can't I get comfortable in this damned seat? Because they were made for hunch-back gnomes, for crissakes. Are you talking to me stewardess?

"You'll have to put your tray in an upright position, sir. We're still on an active taxi-way."

Active, my ass, lady. The only thing active out here is my stomach acid. How about something cold to drink?

"Sorry, we're all out of beverages."

It's 106 damned degrees, no air conditioning, we haven't moved in 50 minutes, and now we face death by dehydration. What's the poker lady doing? Still sleeping. She must be high on drugs. What's with my kidneys? This is the third time in half an hour. What's this? Movement? Yes, we're moving. Finally, we make it to the gate. Swell, now I've got twelve minutes to run to the other end of the world's second largest airport to make my connecting flight. The goddamn Roadrunner on uppers couldn't do it. Where the hell are those motorized courtesy carts with the guy shouting "Beep, beep, coming through," when you need them? Anybody hear a "beep, beep"? No, all right, gotta run for it.

Now, what's going on? Sweating like a honeymooner in August. Chest pains. Forget it, keep running. Just what I need, a goddamn heart attack.

Get out of my way, kid, or so help me, I'll mash you into roadkill. Whew, I'm out of shape. Screw those Stepmasters, not worth a damn. There's the gate. I see it, I see it.

"Hi, sorry for the heavy breathing. I don't know why I ran all the way.

You folks always hold connecting flights when the primary flight is late.

Any chance of getting an aisle seat?"

"I'm sorry, sir, your flight left four minutes ago"

"How the hell can that be? You've got the worst on time departure record in the civilized world. Howcum today you decide to play beat the clock? This airline sucks. You people couldn't find your ass with a rear view mirror. You want me to hold my voice down? Fine, call the goddamned plane back to the gate, and I'll hold my voice down! Who are you?"

"*Airport security, sir. Please calm down or I'll have to remove you from the terminal*"

"Fine, remove me to an airplane, Dick Tracy, so I can get to the most important business meeting of my life, goddammit! Look, I lived up to my end of the bargain. I did everything you asked me to do...I made my reservation 21 days in advance. I showed up at the airport two-and-a-half hours before the flight. I limited myself to one carry on bag and YOU screwed up everything else."

"Sir, if you don't quiet down I'll be forced to put you in restraints. Now, we'll get you on the next available flight, if you'll just mellow out, sit down, and relax."

Okay, okay. I'm sitting. I'm taking deep breaths and I'm mellowing out.

No, I don't believe it, it's her, the lady on the plane. She missed the connection, too. I'll just turn around, maybe she won't see me. Oh damn, she's coming over.

"Hi."

"Hi. I see you missed the connection, too. Say, how did you get here before me. I set a record for the two-thousand-yard dash."

"I took one of those courtesy carts. It came just as you left."

A long, long silence.

"You know, I couldn't help but notice you were a little edgy. Would you like to play a little electronic poker?"

"No, thanks. Really I…"

"I used to be an uptight traveler, too. I tried everything: pills, patches, Zen meditation, frozen daiquiris—nothing worked, but this."

She's taking out her stupid, mindless damned little game.

"Come on, let's play. It's very relaxing."

Sure, lady. Right after they suck the brains out of my head and start force-feeding me Pablum through a straw.

She reads my Captain Hook smirk as a definite, no thank you.

The next available flight is delayed three-and-a-half hours.

I beat her 103 out of 114 hands.

IN PURSUIT OF
STUFF

On January 17, 1994, at 4:31 in the morning, I was unceremoniously flung four-and-a-half feet from my bed through my closet door. Everything in my little cottage by the park that was hanging on the wall or standing on a shelf was now a deadly projectile hurling through the air—crashing, careening, bouncing, exploding into tinier missiles of destruction, glass shattering, soul-wrenching screaming, animals yelping, the ground moving violently beneath me. Make no mistake, disaster has its own symphony. It was here and now—California earthquake.

A big one, 6.7 on the Richter scale, but that figure sheds no real understanding of the devastating power generated. In less than ten seconds, immovable objects moved, like state-of-the art, earthquake-proof, steel reinforced freeways crumbling to white ashen powder. Fifty-five lives were lost; twenty billion dollars worth of damage lies in smoldering rubble; dreams ended; and ten million people looked to the heavens and wondered if a Divine force was finally ending all life on a planet already hell-bent on self-destruction. The equivalent of a two kilo ton atomic bomb had exploded fifteen miles beneath the surface of Southern California.

At this moment, I knew none of these things. It didn't matter, because all terror is local. It happens where you stand, or in this instance where you crawl. My little single-wall, wood-frame cottage built just after Johnny came marching home from World War II was swaying wildly, but rhythmically, east and west, while the earth rumbled with the wail of a giant pterodactyl bellowing in a cave. Fifty-year old plaster was falling all around me like that benign snow in a Currier and Ives painting. I cautiously groped my way in pitch blackness to that celebrated site of salvation we're all trained to find in such calamities—the bathroom doorway. Without warning, a four-by-eight wooden beam came crashing through the ceiling and brushed my left ear. So much for salvation.

I grabbed a hunk of something smooth and solid, held it over my head just as a jagged length of pipe on target to crush my skull slid harmlessly off my new overhead protector. I made a dash to where I thought the front door was. Another avalanche of ceiling debris came tumbling down. Again I escaped serious injury under my umbrella of unknown something. I jumped through where I guessed the front door window was. I guessed right. Safe at last.

When I landed on the front lawn, I immediately kissed my smooth, solid something protector and recorded what I'm sure was the first, and perhaps only, laugh of the Los Angeles Northridge earthquake of '94.

The one still functioning street light gave just enough illumination for me to identify I was holding my solid mahogany toilet seat cover. My Brooklyn mama once told me, "Be kind to all things animate and inanimate. You never know when those people or things will save you from harm." Now, I'm a believer. I will never again enter a privy without feeling a profound sense of gratitude for the sturdy construction of commode covers.

Back in the moment.

I was now lying on the front lawn looking up at the most frighteningly magnificent sight of a lifetime, a giant laser show of light was crisscrossing the sky, converging in a hundred different patterns, and then breaking apart like sub-atomic particles under pressure shooting back to earth in kaleidoscopic thunderbolts only to bounce right back into the suddenly clear winter sky as yet another phantas-magoric display of colliding light and energy. It's what you might expect if all the lightning in a summer storm decide to strike in one place at one time, but this lightning carried no power to harm or sound to frighten. It enlightened rather than destroyed.

What was it?

Was it the calling card of "The Big One" predicted since the middle of the eighteenth century to separate California from the rest of the continent, sinking into the Pacific and lost for all time? Or was it much beyond that? Was it finally Armageddon's prophesy fulfilled? Had the earth stopped spinning on its axis? Were we all being caught up in a final vortex of frenzy that would end our universe forever? Those who have never stood in the epicenter of nature's ultimate devastating force will never understand these terrifying thoughts of final judgment at hand.

The lady in the pink nightgown running up and down the street with her substantial bosoms flopping out of their flimsy restraints understood. She kept yelling, "It's the end of the world. It's the end of the world!"

About two dozen other neighbors in their night clothes agreed with her. They were kneeling in the street, crying, praying, hugging, completely humbled before a mysterious force roaring an absolute power capable of shaking the planet into oblivion. The old lady in the Sesame Street pajamas across the way was convinced the Rapture had come to North Bluffside Drive. Arms stretched out wide like a welcoming archangel, she was blissfully but loudly proclaiming what the gentiles among us were thinking, "It's Jesus, all right. It's Jeees-sus!"

No, it wasn't.

It was the reflection of a full moon bouncing off the hundreds of black tinted windows of the twenty-story Arco Tower a hundred yards away, as it swayed ominously back and forth on its foundation in an eerie synchronization with all the other tall buildings surrounding our Universal Studios neighbor. It's hard to conceive such an earthly phenomenon could produce such Divine possibilities. I scrambled to my feet only to bump into a distraught chap in a green silk kimono and a hair net pacing back and forth exclaiming, "I'm dying...I'm dying. Oh dear God help me." I went to him immediately.

"Where are you hurt? Where?"

"Not me. My crystal knickknacks are gone. Oh, sweet Jesus, this is the end."

Earthquakes bring out strange priorities in Californians.

Soon another compulsion took hold—people running in and out of their homes in a feeding frenzy to save things, all sorts of things, like family albums, stuffed animals, posters, jewelry boxes, video cassettes, and manila envelopes stuffed with, well, you know, stuff.

Suddenly, a familiar voice was topping all the frightening screams around us. Edie, the eighty-year-old good-neighbor widow who lived in the cottage behind me was running up and down the small flowered pathway separating our two rows of residences. "Oh, my God, Art is trapped inside his house. Somebody please help Art." It was fully ten minutes later before dear sweet Miss Edie realized she wasn't wearing a stitch of clothing.

Art Herrington was the congenial seventy-six-year old landlord who hadn't raised the rent on the eight gingerbread cottages for twenty years in deference to his mostly retired senior citizens, who had all become his extended family. He was living alone now in the back cottage since his wife of half a century had died suddenly last month while pruning the red-and-white rhododendrons that ringed our unique patch of greenery in the middle of the city. His suffering was compounded with a variety of ailments that left both his brain and his body partially paralyzed and virtually helpless.

I flagged down three strangers and together we quickly ran to his front door, knocked it down, and found him buried under a collapsed side wall. We placed him in a chair and carried him outside. He remained pleasant, calm, and seemingly more amused than concerned over the mounting chaos. We carried him halfway up the tiny walkway when we were ambushed by Austina, the other elderly widow from cottage No.4.

Life was tragedy for poor old Ms. Gibbs, and the events of the past five minutes were proof positive for her that God had abandoned His creation and the sun would never shine again. She kept up a constant barrage of droning negativity.

"Oh Art, your property is in ruins. You've lost everything you worked for your whole life. It's all gone. You have nothing now."

Just the sort of pick-me-up a dying man needs to hear while sitting in his underwear in the middle of a pile of junk that used to be the sum total of all he possessed. Nevertheless, Art's pleasant smile never left his big, deeply lined leathery face as Austina continued her weepy, woeful condolences all the way to the front lawn where we placed him down out of harm's way.

Finally, he looked up to her and spoke two simple sentences that stunned us all into a reflective silence that moved the moment to a higher place of understanding. He said, "I was a Marine at Guadalcanal. After that, this is all just, you know, small stuff."

There were eighty-six aftershocks that eventful day, and each one seemed to humble us all just a little more than the last one and strengthen our perspective on what is and is not really important in the face of calamity. But I suspect none taught us more than those simple words spoken by an aging Marine sitting, smiling amid the rubble of the most insignificant of all we possess, you know, stuff.

THE SECOND
SURPRISE ATTACK
ON PEARL HARBOR

Dewey Ramonola was throwing around hundred dollar bills like Mardi Gras confetti, and loving every minute of it. First, the tall, thin, serious haole maitre d' at the outdoor garden of the Royal Monarch Room got one, then the startled Samoan bus boy got one for just pouring water, then the bright, pudgy Filipino waiter got one for just saying, "Good evening, sir, welcome to the Royal Hawaiian Hotel."

Dewey looked out at the white, glistening sands of Waikiki Beach just a few feet away and raised his face just enough to catch the cool touch of the Trades winding around Diamond Head. Oblivious to the waiter's spirited explanation of the recommended menu specials, he inhaled slowly, the way you do when you get close to a big yellow rose.

This was a very special moment, and nothing was to be missed—the full moon painting a dozen shades of silver on a lazy Pacific, the gentle ambling of four-foot waves, giddy, barefooted lovers walking hand-in-hand under the spell of another picture-perfect evening in paradise, and off to the west, past Magic Island and around Kewalo Basin, the sleek, gray silhouette of a ship of the line exiting Pearl Harbor and taking its first pitch and roll from the surf line.

This was to be the beginning of Dewey's greatest adventure…and his last.

"Sir, are you all right?", the waiter asked.

"I'm terrific, young man. Never felt better in my life."

That wasn't quite accurate. There was a grapefruit-size carcinoma sitting in the middle of his large intestine sending out deadly emissaries to every major organ of his body. Doc McLaren, at Kaiser Hospital in Santa Rosa, gave him six months at best. That deadline passed three weeks ago. Now, only those big yellow pills in the red bottle and a dream were keeping him going.

"I'd like one of everything on this menu and three of your best wines, and please give this to the orchestra leader and tell him to play that song again."

For the third time, the bald-headed man with the baton graciously accepted the big bill, waved to Dewey and repeated the most Hawaiian of Hawaiian songs, "To You, Sweetheart, Aloha."

It was the last song of the evening played by the Royal Hawaiian Band on this date, sitting on this very stage fifty three year ago, Saturday, December 6, 1941. The band leader had no idea of its historical significance. Dewey did. He knew that and every other face, fact, and event that played a part in the fateful Day of Infamy that followed the next day and changed the world forever.

Dewey was three years old that day, playing with all the fun stuff in his grandmother's bottom drawer in the kitchen. That's where she kept all her memories and a lot of toys as well. Then it happened. Somebody said something on the big Stromberg Carlson radio in the living room, and grandma dropped her big black pot, the one she made her tomato sauce in. She grabbed her grandson tightly, "Oh, Dewey, they bombed Pearl Harbor. Let's pray for your daddy and all the other boys in service."

Grandma didn't know then that the oldest of her seven sons, Dewey's father, Gunner's Mate First Class, Arthur Louis Ramonola, was already one of the first casualties of World War II, trapped alongside the powder magazine five decks below the Number 2 forward gun turret aboard the *U.S.S. Arizona*.

From that moment on, Dewey's dream remained the same—to grow up to be a hero like his dad, to be part of a sweeping victory over evil like the one faced in that war.

Like the dreams of most kids in that special time of crisis and romance, Dewey didn't come close to reaching it. Too young for WW II and Korea and too old for Vietnam, his road to glory always remained just beyond the reach of his rather ordinary life as an assistant copy editor at the *Santa Rosa Times*.

But always there was Pearl Harbor. Reading everything written about it, interviewing survivors from both sides and, without interruption, visiting the Arizona Memorial every December 7 since its opening in 1962. He would stand at the railing opposite the gaping hole where a 1700 pound converted artillery shell fell ten thousand feet from a Japanese bomber sinking the mighty warship in less than nine minutes, with the greatest loss of life ever suffered by a U.S. Navy ship. Because of the danger posed from acetylene torches igniting trapped gases, divers could not retrieve the Arizona dead. They remain inside her sealed hull, lying where they fell, forever young in a watery grave.

His ritual never changed. Peer down through the still oily water to a point thirty feet below, where he imagined his father's body to be resting. He'd try to remember his big round smiling face, how his whole body shook when he laughed, how the big muscles in his arms would pop up when he hugged him, and his Mom every time he came home from the sea.

Dewey ate most of the keawe grilled mahi-mahi, sampled portions of the white wine poached opakapaka and chateaubriand, sipped a few glasses of Montrachet '85, left another round of hefty tips, and retired to the Presidential Suite on the third floor.

He stood on the balcony of Hawaii's oldest and grandest hotel listening for its secrets. They came. President Franklin D. Roosevelt chatting with his confidant and assistant, Harry Hopkins, about his upcoming Pacific war strategy talks with Admiral Nimitz; Amelia Earhart contemplating her early morning take-off for the final leg of her around-the-world trip; Colonel Tom Parker and Elvis Presley putting the final touches on his upcoming benefit concert to build a memorial over the sunken *Arizona*, a concert that would arouse so much sentiment and publicity that Congress finally appropriated the money to complete the project. And now, Dewey Ramonola, widower and retired small-town journalist, alone with his thoughts of growing up in a long ago time of patriotism, ideals, and hope. He stood watching the full moon slide over to the center of the island and listened to the roll and thunder of the waves crashing on the coral heads a few hundred yards from the beach below, until a constant companion got out of hand and drove him to his knees. The pain was sharper and lingered longer than ever before.

As he reached for the red bottle in his side pocket, he prayed, "Dear God, not now. Please give me just a few hours more." He popped three big yellow pills into his mouth and laid down on the balcony floor anticipating that numbing sensation in his stomach that told him he would be granted another short reprieve from pain.

He did what he always did on these agonizing vigils, he sang songs of the forties. usually, one was all he needed to get him through. Not tonight. He went through "Apple Blossom Time," "White Cliffs of Dover," and three choruses of "Bless Them All" before he could manage to pull himself up.

He took out an old cigar box from his luggage and carefully checked the contents: one pair of handcuffs, a neatly typed letter to the Commandant, Naval Base, Pearl Harbor; a White Owl panatella cigar; a faded black-and-white picture of his family; and a letter from his father promising to take him on a ride aboard his ship. He placed it on the night stand alongside his bed, left a 2:00AM wake-up call and fell off to sleep.

A light mist was falling as Dewey's cab drove through a desserted downtown Honolulu. His sumo-sized Hawaiian driver was skeptical. He had never taken anybody to the airport service road alongside Keehi Lagoon at 2:15 in the morning. But then again, he had never before received a hundred dollar tip just for showing up.

The historic red light district of Hotel Street was surprisingly intact from it's pre-war honky tonk years, as the resting place for a string of raucous gin joints on the ground floor and anything goes bawdy houses above. With a hundred and twenty-five thousand homesick Army, Navy, Marine, and Air Corps personnel crowded onto an island twenty-five by forty miles, it was an irresistibly tacky Sodom and Gomorrah in flashing neon, where the good times rolled twenty-four hours a day. Gone were the legendary sin palaces with names like Tantalizing Tootsie's, Hotsy Totsie's Cave of Pleasure, and Big Fat Red Hot Mama's but their ghosts were still lurking in the oriental herb shops, chop suey parlors and lei stands that now occupied their spaces.

"Did you know at this time in the morning on December 7, 1941, over six thousand servicemen were walking these streets?" Dewey muttered to no one in particular.

"Yeah, Bruddah. My far'der and my uncle was one of 'dem. Nickle Beer Night. Hawaiians nevah pass up a bargain, you know," the driver responded with a good-natured laugh.

As they turned off Nimitz Highway and swung down toward the harbor, the driver inquired, "Where you want me to drop you off, Mistah?"

Dewey checked the note from Cap Aluli and responded, "All the way to the end until you see three baby palm trees."

The driver slowed down, as there was little left of the full moon to illuminate the way. To the left, in sad contrast to the huddled skyscrapers of modern Honolulu off in the distance, was Keehi Lagoon, an eerie graveyard of rusting, half-submerged scows, houseboats, freighters, and flatbed barges sticking up from the mud at ghostly angles like so many condemned souls pleading for salvation. To the right was the pitch darkness of the new airport reef runway, a necessary addition to an expanding visitor industry.

Suddenly, a giant roar exploded overhead as a 747 lifted into the night. Its four thrusting engines rattled the cab's window and shook loose the plastic Jesus from the sun-baked dashboard. As it banked to the west, a sliver of moonbeam bounced off the unmistakable insignia on the fuselage, the blood red ball of the rising sun.

The driver shakes his fist at the plane and exclaims, "Damn Japanese are taking over dis' place. Makes me sick." He paused, looked in the rear view mirror and added, "I guess dey found da' bomb dat works, money!"

He didn't wait for a reply, he laughed unpretensiously as Dewey acknowledged the irony with a nod. Japanese interests own ninety-three percent of Hawaii's tourist industry, while the sons and daughter of Nippon comprise one out of every three of the island's six-and-a-half million annual visitors.

They pull up at three baby palm trees just short of a barbed wired fence.

The happiest cabbie in Polynesia receives another hundred dollar bill and speeds off in the blackness shouting a hearty "Alooooha."

Dewey checks the note again. "Meet you at the brown brick house at the end of the concrete pier."

Dewey always was a great judge of character, and had no doubts the old man at the marina boat shop would deliver on his promises.

He did.

He was there at the far piling with a seven-foot wooden rowboat, two-and-a-half horse powered outboard motor, two oars, a ten-gallon tank of gas and a word of caution, "Eeet's none of my business, Mistah', you paid for everyting,' but wherever you going tonight, be careful. Dees tides are tough, if you don't know dis' ocean."

Dewey had never put to sea in these waters, but he had carefully studied the navigational charts of southern Oahu since he was seven years old. He knew every shoal, sandbar, and riptide in the area. He had prepared well for this moment. He handed the old man a white envelope bulging with hundred dollar bills at about the same time it stopped raining. The old man looked up to the heavens and offered, "You know, u'a (rain) is the Hawaiian gods' blessing on whatever you're goin' to do dis' day."

Dewey waited until the old man's car was out of sight to cast off and begin his incredible odyssey. He put his cigar box on the deck of the boat beside him and took a deep breath, the way climbers looking up at the top of their mountains do before taking their first step. The air was crisp, clean, and filled with the fragrance of the tropics, white ginger, frangipani and a hint of plumeria. He took out a little blue notebook, paused, and then made an entry:

> Ship's log—USS Remembrance 0231. The second sneak attack on Pearl Harbor begins. Cool night, little moonlight, making my way against the current. Plan six legs to destination: east to the tip of the reef runway, then north a half mile to open water. Turn west for three miles hugging the shoreline until I reach Hickam Harbor, then north by northwest for 2.2 miles to the entrance of Pearl. Proceed 1.2 miles inside the harbor to Hospital Point. Will lay to until 0345, and then continue to Quay # 7 on Battleship Row. Fifty-three years ago this date, thirty six ships sailed 4,000 miles over open water undetected by the US military. They used the element of surprise. I intend to do the same.

Dewey knew the odds were against him. In 1941 radar detection was very primitive, but not today. He would have to elude the Star Wars electronic surveillance of the Coast Guard, Air Force, U.S. Navy, and the Honolulu Harbor Police. Still, he had a feeling the idea was so preposterous that with a little luck he just might pull off this final adventure. Human nature and history were on his side. During the original attack, monumental oversights coupled with plain bureaucratic fumbling combined to unwittingly insure a Japanese success. The destroyer Ward encountered and sunk a Japanese midget submarine at the entrance to Pearl fully one hour before the attack and radioed the warning to fleet headquarters, where subordinates shuffled the report back and forth finally reaching the base commander twenty minutes before the bombs fell. Two conscientious nineteen-year-old radar operators at the Opana Point station on the northern tip of Oahu detected the approaching wave of attacking planes, but were told by the first-time duty officer with no prior watch experience, "They're probably ours. Shut off the radar and go to breakfast." There were two months of intercepted Japanese messages that, when pieced together, clearly pointed to possible hostile action against the Pacific Fleet, but no one stepped forward to see the big picture forming. The Day of Infamy happened because human nature was unable to think the unthinkable even when it came knocking on the door.

Dewey was banking on human fallibility. It happened before, it could happen again. His plan was to make the six point seven miles to Pearl by 3:45 AM. That was the time the most unpopular watch in the military came on duty, the early morning dog watch. He remembered his own Navy days, how bleary-eyed and dull his brain was several minutes before acclimating to pre-dawn consciousness. That's the moment he'd seize, when sleepy eyes don't focus very well on radar screens to see a seven-foot row boat breaching the security of America's most powerful Pacific naval base.

The tide was much stronger than he anticipated and he struggled to keep his barely adequate craft from broaching as it plowed into choppy waters alongside the artificial reef runway. If he could just make the 1200 yards to the channel before another monster jet boomed into the night, he'd avoid being capsized by its 48,000 pounds of thrust and pick up a following current, which would keep him on time for his incredible rendezvous.

Like a leaf in a wind tunnel, the *USS Remembrance* was tossed and bruised by an ornery winter ocean hellbent on turning it into another afterthought, like all the other abandoned remnants ringing the lagoon.

Suddenly, a violent wind sweeping around the point sent a wall of water into the boat threatening to sent her to the muddy bottom. With one hand on the tiller, Dewey ripped off a shoe and used it to bail. Only a hundred more yards to the protected channel and calm water. As the boat lightened, it picked up speed and was moving closer to safe haven, when the paralyzing thunder of a thousand screeching airborne chariots shot through the hovering darkness behind him. The ear-bursting sonic boom created a giant fist that pounded ocean and coastline into frightened submission and sent Dewey sprawling forward onto the wet deck. Another jumbo jet was announcing its departure from terra firma. Roaring just a few feet overhead, it was on target to deliver the coup de gras to the impossible voyage below.

Dewey always recognized the comedy in all pain, and this moment was no different from the time six months ago when Doc McLaren told him he was terminal. He'd turned to the somber faced medic and exclaimed with great gusto, "Thank God, Doc. I thought it was gas." He could still see the startled expression on the confused good doctor's face, and was laughing out loud when the 747 catapulted overhead kicking up a series of mini-tidal waves below.

"Dammit! The Japanese didn't have this much trouble in '41. Why me, Lord? What's next, a freakin' typhoon?"

He was still grinning at the irony when he reached the leeward side of Kalihi Channel and headed around the end of the runway toward the ocean.

Outside the channel he picked up a friendly current and a warm, soft trade wind that relieved the strain on his tiny outboard engine and effortlessly pushed him the three miles west toward Hickam Harbor alongside the naval base.

Log entry:

> 0306 One mile at sea directly south of Hickam Air Force Base at the entrance to Pearl Harbor. Haven't seen anything move except sand crabs on the shoreline and those damn noisy Jap tourist planes overhead. So far, so good. Now, the hard part—leg #4, 2.2 miles to Iroquois Point opposite the West Loch Naval Magazine and a restricted security zone. If I'm going to go down in flames, this is most likely the place.

He closed the book, took off his jacket, and put it over the outboard motor to muffle the stuttering "put-put" sound and give him a final advantage as he entered the narrow channel leading to the most famous harbor in world history.

Now he felt it as he had so many times before—the unmistakable reverence in the air, a special eternal benediction shared with Gettysburg, the Normandy Beaches, and the Mount at Calvary. Little had changed here since that fateful day five decades ago. Every old military gray building, every corrugated tin roof and Quonset hut, every pock-marked limestone observation tower and airplane hangar, many still showing .50-caliber machine gun holes, beat out a constant tattoo:

"This is a special place. Honor the memory, or be doomed to repeat it."

As Dewey slid by the spot where the *USS Ward* fired the first offensive shot of World War II, a paralyzing chill shot through his body and awakened an angry voice within, "What's wrong with you, Dewey? What gives you the right to invade the sanctity of this place? Your dying has nothing to do with the heroic sacrifices that bless these waters."

He answered the voice out loud, "I know I belong here. I've known it all my life. All pilgrims come to that place in their mind that is finally home.

And this is mine. I will do this thing."

Log entry:

0347 Astern Drydock No.4 at the shipyard. I can see Ford Island and the Arizona Memorial just a few hundred yards ahead. How have I been able to come this far undetected? Maybe hugging the shoreline preventing a radar blip, I don't know. Why didn't duty sentries make a visual sighting? Can an old man in a leaky row boat do what no other ship and her master have been able to do in 53 years—breach the security of Pearl Harbor? So much for high-tech surveillance.

Suddenly, Dewey grabbed his stomach in great pain. His dark visitor was attacking on all fronts, deeper and more complete than ever before. His hands were stinging with a pulsating numbness that left them useless, dangling aimlessly at his side like severed tree branches in a high wind. Life was leaving his body, and there was nothing he could do about it. The red bottle with the big yellow pills were a thousand miles away in his pants pocket. He collapsed in an inch of smelly oily water on the deck.

"My God," he thought, I'm losing consciousness. I can't let this happen. I'm too close. Please, dear God, help me...don't sit under the apple tree with anyone else but me, anyone else but me...."

He lay helpless in the early morning chill, his crippled body shivering with excruciating pain.

This day a pathetic fading murmur would greet the fifty-fourth anniversary of the most significant event of the twentieth century.

"Please, God, please."

He didn't lose consciousness, but that was feeble consolation. He could move nothing. His life was no longer his own. An army of cancerous microbes deep inside had severed all lines of control and were massing for a final assault. His inert body rocked back and forth in the foul bilge water to the rhythm of the incoming tide. Soon the familiar sound of reveille would blare throughout the harbor and awaken the Pacific Fleet to a day of remembrance and ceremony, and a pitiful old man in a sinking rowboat would be discovered a few hundred yards from his final dream.

That thought played over and over again inside Dewey's brain until the miracles men make took over.

"I've still got my will, and that's enough," he thought.

Like some ancient mantra with the power to move the unmovable, he kept repeating the words, "Yes, I will, yes, I will," until the death grip of his unrelenting tormentor slowly loosened under the constant barrage of determination. Who knows why or how these things happen, but the power of a single act of will was rising mightily and resurrecting a life in the murky waters behind Drydock No. 4 in Pearl Harbor. Dewey had no strength but he had movement, and maybe that was enough. He had lost precious time. He had to find a way to restart the motor and make a straight-line run alongside Ford Island to the *Arizona* before the sun came up.

"Now, you only have one shot at this. Let's make it good, Dewey, old boy."

He threw his body against the outboard motor and grabbed the starter cord in both hands. He took a deep breath and whispered, "I need your help, Dad," and hurled himself backwards. Cap Aluli's brand new Evinrude "put-put" answered immediately. The *USS Remembrance* was underway again. Dewey could see the first slivers of light peeking over Kole Kole Pass and bouncing off the white marble memorial spanning the sunken Arizona just ahead.

He passed permanently vacant moorings where once great giants berthed—the battleships *California, Maryland, Oklahoma, West Virginia* and *Tennessee.*

Suddenly his journey was over. He was alongside the Arizona Memorial.

The engine sputtered and went silent. He peered through the long marble hall to the darkened shrine room wall at the other end where the names of all 1,177 men entombed below are inscribed. His memory saw what his eyes could not, a clear picture of the twelfth column, fifth name from the top—Ramonola, Arthur GM1.

He opened his waterlogged cigar box, found his father's letter, and put it in his shirt pocket. He looked at his family picture and smiled, "Sorry, Pop, I was going to smoke that cigar you sent me, but...I just couldn't keep my powder or my matches dry."

He picked up the handcuffs and snapped one clip to his left wrist.

He looked around the sleeping harbor one last time and then down below the surface to the clear outline of *BB 39, USS ARIZONA*.

As he let the boat drift a few feet aft of the memorial toward the submerged gun turret No.2, he thought out loud, "For all the blood and carnage, it was still a good time to live. A time of purpose, a time when all things noble were possible, a time for heroes. I loved that time."

A light rain started falling. Dewey lifted his face to catch a few drops, took a deep breath, leaned forward, and let gravity take him over the side. He disappeared under the surface descending slowly to a torn railing beside the gun turret. Marshalling his final effort, he clamped the other handcuff shut around a twisted mounting at the base.

The pain was gone. Dewey Ramonola felt nothing but contentment. He was young again. He was home.

CARPE DIEM EX NIHILO

The older I get the more I realize you can[1] *carpe diem* sometimes by just doing nothing, not the foreboding nothing of Sartre or the nineteenth century bloody nihilism of Russian politics or any post-pubescent teenager, which is always the absence of something, but rather the rhythmic nothingness of nature, homeostasis, all things balanced in their natural flow.

You know what I'm talking about: that unexcited euphoria you feel on the front porch on a lazy Sunday afternoon after you've read the papers and can't detect an urge to do anything but sit and let your eyes wander; the nothingness of a ship swaying effortlessly on its anchor chain; a baby in his carriage looking up at the soft tapestry of the sky with no intent diluting the moment; a daydreamer without an image; a leaf obeying the push and pull of a wind; a simple pure act of being without the possibility of urgency.

It's a blasphemous state for the modern mind-bending crowd that adores at the altar of achievement and insists redemption is a transitive

---

1. *seize the day*

verb, a self-starting homing missile with a pre-programmed flight path, kinetic energy, a purpose and, of course, the ultimate goal of all their activity—a target. To them, the antithesis is either chaos or a slow-drip degeneration into a black hole of self-loathing and mediocrity.

They see no beauty in the forming of clouds, only in the end result, which is always a sham, because clouds are never complete, never on target to become a definitive something. They, like all forces in nature, but a lot faster than most, are amorphous, constantly swirling from one boundless form to another. Like the hands of a clock, they are never at one point at one time. There is no *now* because you can not stop what is in perpetual motion. Yes, there is formative activity in the life of clouds, but there is also a lot of nothingness going on. It is precisely that nothingness that gives them their grandeur and dominion over all definite things below.

Consider this, not one recorded philosophy was ever birthed through syllogistic logic, including St. Thomas' celebrated five proofs for the existence of a Supreme Being. Even the brilliant Dominican theologian readily admitted they appeared in completed self-evident whispers from the small still voice within, clearly spontaneous combustion, not logarithmic effort and process.

To the ancient Chinese, nothingness was the ultimate state of being because it was the only moment in life in which the mind was truly open, unfettered by history and pedestrian bias, and available for the visitation of primal understanding, the beginning of all serviceable knowledge. It was all about creating quiet reception, cleaning the blackboard of your mind to allow the universal force to write upon your slate.

This is not to be confused with meditation, which is a guide, a process for contemplation, *a something*, and something only interferes with nothingness. It follows that nothingness must also be the starting point for peace of mind, if you define it as a balance of all we know we are and a static contentment we are moving to what we can be. Balance is nature's nothingness, its uneventful acceptance of all activity of genesis and death that has brought us to this moment where cause and effect are one, neither waiting nor anticipating calamity, change, or energy. It is simply the now, possessing all the ingredients for meaningful life we need to rise higher in our personal evolution, if only we will go quietly into nothingness where all things are revealed.

Emerson said transitions should be natural, unforced. I never understood that, for I am modern man, Gemini to boot, filled with seven generations of a culture forged in adversity and solely supported by the notion of constant achievement toward a better tomorrow for self and country. Isn't my job to be constantly overcoming, innovating, climbing to a new plateau? Aren't those activities the process for all gains, physical and spiritual? Isn't progress the Divine imperative and *carpe diem* the tattoo of a valued life?

I thought so up to this wonderfully strange, confusing moment in my fifty-sixth year of life, but now I find no solace in all the precepts of forward motion that got me here. And I'm not sure why. Is it, simply, I've outgrown my dream or perhaps my dream, like the dreams of all long-distance runners, was never real to begin with? My new metaphysics dictates it really doesn't matter, because I can't find the answer in doing anything.

My passion is gone, and passion is the engine of achievement. Without it, any activity, any movement to search for your next step is counterproductive.

For the first time in my life, I suspect I must do what has never occurred to me before—retreat for a moment into nothingness and allow all that I am and all that nature in me is—and regain the balance that surely comes to every morsel, living or inert, when it seeks merely to be and not to become.

I'm smiling the smile of the wily old magician who announces he is going to do the impossible, knowing full well he has practiced the trick a thousand times and there is nothing left to surprise him. I know myself and my talents and the definite flow of my life. How can doing nothing reveal any new directions to me?

Ah, but that is the wrong question to ask. Nay, there should be no questions asked when you enter this natural state of nothingness.

There are no questions and no answers in this boundless place, just the balance of your being that puts you at one with the condition for learning all that you need to learn.

I have come so far and reached so high for so long and now feel empty, but perhaps with a new understanding of nothingness, I can end all that in a land of no expectation. Perhaps.

"A man," said Oliver Cromwell, "never rises so high as when he knows not wither he is going."

I am on a mountaintop.

THE HEALING
ROOM

St. Mary's Medical Center on the corner of Stanyan and Folsum
Streets in the Golden Gate Park section of San Francisco served the
working poor of their blue-collar neighborhood faithfully, and usually,
without remuneration, for ninety-three years. But while their charity
was legend, their economics were pitiful. Plagued by creditors who
didn't share their ideal of care now, pay later if you can, the Sisters of
the Sacred Heart were forced to close the big, red cedar-front doors for
good. That was five years ago. Now, beaten down by the wind, van-
dals, and a constant flow of marauding drug dealers, the six-story
brown brick, hulking shell Mother Theresa once hailed as "America's
finest beacon of hope" was in shambles. The bankruptcy court, in deference to the Sisters' constant faith a financial angel would appear and
rescue their work, delayed the inevitable. Now there would be no more
reprieves. The building, 3.2 acres of land, three gutted ambulances,
and the meager contents of the building would go to the highest bidder
Thursday morning at nine, but the winning bid would get much more
than prime real estate. They would soon become the benefactors of the
most astonishing chapter in the history of medicine, a process so pro-

found and mystical in its consequences as to slow the very tempo of evil in the world and turn all eyes toward the City by the Bay.

Charmian Kettering, CEO of National Hospital Enterprises, the largest hospital conglomerate in the world, didn't know that when the court referee announced her closed bid of 21.8 million dollars had beaten out Budget Rent-A-Car and Walmart for the sweetest land grab since the Louisiana Purchase.

Four years ago, the "Blond Shark", as she was cautiously called by her peers, had performed financial magic and brought NHE from the brink of collapse to the undisputed kingpin of international health care. She reveled in defying the entrenched starchy wisdom of a profession notorious for anchoring its feet in the past. While the rest of modern health care reeled in a stifling quandary under the impossible restraints of a new economy demanding more for less, NHE was in bullish overdrive, buying real estate, erecting newer, highly innovative ventures that had earned them the epithet, "The Star Wars Hospital Chain."

There was the Space Medicine Hospital in Ogden capitalizing on NASA discoveries and convincing a gullible public in search of immortality that a high-tech state-of-the-art hospital with futuristic technology housed in a phantasmagoric maze of interconnected tunnels and Flash Gordon geometry somehow came with a guaranteed cure for all that ails you. There was the Genetic Correction Medical Center in Dallas, where somber-faced geneticists in sterile space suits worked in glass monoliths, tampering and rearranging the DNA of life to thwart paralysis, deformity, disease, and even death.

The AMA was outraged, but an enthralled public demanded new perceptions of healing, and nobody engineered public perceptions better than the NHE brain trust. An unprecedented two-for-one stock split four years in a row had drowned out all critics of their glitzy promotional approach to medical intervention. In a new age of "packaging" dreams, NHE was the quintessential dream maker, and Charmian Kettering was its Merlin.

She bounded into the white marble board room with her usual lofty arrogance, thinly disguised as a gracious zeal, and declared, "Ladies and gentlemen, today we are bringing America and the world into a new, brighter age of medical excellence." That last word caused Dr. David LeCouer, staff director of Medical Ethics, to squirm noticeably in his chair. Charmian paused long enough to shoot him a piercing look of disapproval and then continued, "With the purchase of St. Mary's, we have a superior piece of land in the heart of what soon will be the most modernized redeveloped city area in the country, the perfect setting for…" she paused and then in one sweeping, dramatic moment pulled the white cover off the model in the center of the table revealing a series of gleaming crystal-domed spheres seemingly suspended in space, "NHE's MEDILARK, the new, exciting world of breakthroughs. MEDILARK, where the most brilliant medical technicians meet the most advanced technologies in every healing science under the sun." Her eyes narrowed as her voice reached a high-pitched intensity that beat down her audience's incredulity by the sheer power of its conviction.

"Think of it. The best medical science has to offer under one roof, so to speak—cancer research, state-of-the-art trauma wards, advanced laser technology, every conceivable surgery brought to its highest degree of efficiency, all side by side routinely producing the impossible, and immediately satelliting the results around the globe." Her passion danced on the edge of frenzy like an avenging angel invoking a new order. "Every patient in the world who has the least doubt about his condition won't hesitate. We'll eliminate all other options. They must come to us, because here we'll produce miracles. Very simply, ladies and gentlemen, MEDILARK will not lead the world of medicine into the future, MEDILARK will be the future."

Stunned, motionless silence.

Finally, David LeCouer unceremoniously broke the paralysis. "Kind of a one-stop shopping center for the sick and dying, a super medical

K-Mart for the Star Trek generation. Isn't that what we're talking about here, Ms. Kettering?"

He didn't give her a chance to respond. His smiling outrage was on a roll. Pointing to the model and an intricate railway system ringing the project, he continued the attack, "And what are these cute little Disneyland trams with all these cute Lilliputians inside? Don't tell me, let me guess. Organ donors on their way to NHE's Transplant World where Mickey, Minnie, and Donald will remove their kidneys, lungs, and hearts six times a day, matinee performances Saturday and Sunday. For God's sake, this isn't medicine. It's the ultimate half-time show at the Super Bowl."

A long pause ensued, as all eyes shifted to Charmian. She was used to the intense academician's opposition, and was never phased by it. She lived in another world, where traditional ethics were never a match for modern consumerism. She always held four aces.

She calmly pointed to the railway network.

"These are tourist trams. They'll carry 1.8 million people a year paying 56.7 million dollars to witness the latest miracles in alleviating pain and prolonging the quality of life. That money will pay the salaries for the most advanced research in the history of the world, create more hope and eradicate more suffering than all the healing that ever was. She lowered her voice to a whisper and continued, "You can call it show business, David. I prefer to think of it as funding the greatest humane project on the planet."

The nodding heads around him signified the obvious. LeCouer was outgunned again. He gathered his notes and left.

While the rest of the meeting would be consumed with dazzling multi-media images of MEDILARK, it was a small matter at the end of the session that drew very little notice, but would forever relegate the revolutionary project to a feeble footnote.

Dr. Kastan Rastiti, Staff Medical Director, suggested the fifth-floor operating room in St. Mary's be refitted for the six months prior to demolition and used to handle the overload at two of NHE's downtown hospitals. "I've checked the room and it's in remarkable condition. I'm sure we could get certification immediately." It was beyond remarkable, it defied logic. While the rest of the complex was victimized by rust, age, and vandalism, the room that had served popes and paupers since the turn of the century had somehow remained shiny, spotless, untouched, frozen in an eerie perfection.

Within two weeks, it was in full use, but at the end of the first day's operations, it was dramatically clear something was quite wrong.

Rastiti shook his head in disbelief, as he slowly dropped the day's OR report on Charmian's desk.

"It doesn't make any sense; it makes no sense at all."

Charmian read aloud, "Fourteen-and-a-half-hour period, five operations: a hip replacement, an appendectomy, two carpel tunnels, and a rhinoplasty. Seems quite routine to me, doctor."

The veteran physician kept shaking his head. Finally, he sat down and said in a very low voice, "Far from routine. Two of those patients died. Simple non-life threatening procedures performed with textbook accuracy, yet we lost them." Charmian's legendary cool was leaving.

"Good Christ. Just what we need, two major malpractice suites the day before we announce MEDILARK."

"There was no malpractice, dammit," Restiti angrily replied, "We did everything letter perfect. Post-op vital signs were normal. Each patient was in excellent condition with no prior major health problems, yet, the moment we pushed them out the door, they just…stopped breathing for no medical reason at all."

"Well, if it wasn't surgeon error, then what are we looking at here, another Legionnaire's Disease, alien spores in the air conditioning ducts, what?"

What indeed.

All operations in the room were halted, while a blue ribbon team of biochemists, environmental engineers, and disease-control specialists combed every square inch of old St. Mary's rejuvenated fifth floor OR.

They not only found the space free of any lethal organisms, but declared it one hundred percent fit for duty.

Two surgeons were placed on indefinite suspension, and the OR reopened for business.

Fifteen operations were performed in three days without incident, and then on the fourth day, at 7:45 AM, a robbery suspect with a bullet wound to his left thigh died mysteriously moments after being wheeled out of surgery.

Again, there were investigations, again, no explanation was found. Then that afternoon while Dr. Charles Vensolving, one of the world's foremost brain surgeons was debriefing his team after successfully performing a cryothalamectomy—a delicate probe deep inside the thalamus where a targeted area is frozen dead in hopes of restoring motor skills impaired by Parkinson's Syndrome—his chief nurse, Barbara Nehoa, burst in with uncustomary emotion, grabbed the surgeon's arm, and demanded he return to OR immediately.

"Come quickly, Doctor. You're not going to believe this. Oh, my God!"

Fearing post-operative shock, the entire team quickly resuited and ran back into the operating room, where the patient, a very serene looking fifty-eight year old female was resting comfortably on the OR table.

Dr. Vensolving deftly checked all her vital signs and declared his patient in good condition.

Nurse Nehoa was close to hysteria as she shouted, "Her right leg, check her right leg, doctor."

He did.

"There's nothing wrong with her right leg, nurse. Now why all this commotion…" She didn't let him finish and was frantically shaking the patient's chart in his face.

"That's just it. Mrs. Moreno is—was—an amputee. She didn't have a right leg when she came in here. Oh, my God! What's happening?"

The happening didn't stop there. Forty-five minutes later, in the same room, on the same table in pre-op preparation, Daniel J. Moumulian, a seventy-three-year old blind cancer patient regained full vision and subsequently tested free of the grapefruit size colorectal growth that was ending his life. That afternoon, a four-year-old hemophiliac, who had contacted the HIV virus through a contaminated blood transfusion, shocked his surgical team, waking up seconds after being injected with 20cc's of Fentanyl, a powerful anesthetic, and declaring he was fine. A hematology sample proved just how fine he was. The deadly virus had simply, inexplicably, disappeared.

On and on it went. Limbs reappeared, speech and hearing was restored, and something else—two more unexplained deaths with no conceivable doctor error at all.

Why was this happening? The world wanted to know. Medical science wanted to know. War, corruption, greed, famine, strife, and all the other incessant evils that demean us all abruptly left the front pages. The earth was still spinning on its axis, gravity was still moving the solar system, but there was a universal quiet that overshadowed all human and natural physics. The *Berlin Daily News* featured a front-page picture of an undistinguished, humble, fading building on the West Coast of America and filled the rest of the space with a unanimous common sentiment:

> It is as if a cosmic giant has called "time out" and the game, all games, are temporarily suspended. We all continue to live, to work and eat and sleep, but in subdued insignificance, for all eyes are turned to a very special room in a dilapidated relic that once was St. Mary's Hospital in San Francisco. Something strange and wonderful is happening here, something beyond intelligence, that once in a millennium mystical fascination that draws every human heart, good or bad, to the Divine spark in all things, hope.

The world was waiting for an answer.

Charmian listened impatiently, as one by one her senior management team reported their findings of investigations that led nowhere, proved nothing, drew no conclusions. Science had no empirical data to explain the spontaneous generation of limbs, the disappearance of virulent cancer in a final stage, and life springing from death.

Dr. Rastiti nervously paced back and forth in front of a large wall chart.

"Thirty-one operations, seven unexplained deaths, fifteen normal recoveries and nine..." he paused as the words stuck in his throat.

Dr. LeCouer finished the sentence, "...miracles. Go ahead, doctor, say it, because that's what we're dealing with here. *Miracle*, from the latin *mirari*—to wonder at. An extraordinary event manifesting Divine intervention in human affairs."

The young, dedicated ethician tore a sheet of paper from a file and stood up. "Miracles of this magnitude, while sporadic, do not occur out of happenstance. They come for a very real, special purpose, usually at a critical turning point in history. On the eve of World War I in 1917, the Blessed Virgin appeared in a grotto in Fatima in central Portugal to three shepherd children and warned them the world was in imminent danger. There are a dozen more authenticated incidents of Divine apparitions all over the globe on the eve of massive evil." He paused as if listening to the echo of his own words. "I think we can all agree that mankind is once again teetering on the edge of the abyss. The question now is, what are these miracles trying to tell us?"

"And I assume you have the answer, Doctor", Charmian smugly interjected. "No, I don't," said LeCouer, "but I do know what's happening."

The fifteen board members froze in unison.

LeCouer picked up an orange folder, "The answer isn't in the patient's medical history. It's in the lives they lead." He placed the folder on the table and slowly moved it in front of Charmian.

"One career criminal, two chronic wife abusers, a drug dealer, a priest under scrutiny for child molestation..."

Charmian pounded the table to make a point, "If all this is some kind of celestial retribution, how do you account for the death of Mr. Dalton Carmody, one of the most respected investment bankers in the country?"

LeCouer slowly, purposely pulled a newspaper clipping from his briefcase and handed it to Charmian. "Mrs. Barbara Carmody, his estranged wife, yesterday told the Securities and Exchange Commission her former husband has been skimming substantial amounts of money from the bank's four largest mutual fund accounts for years."

More silence.

Finally, LeCouer continued, "The bottom line is that whatever force controls that room has a flawless sense of good and evil."

Dr. Rastiti quietly finished the thought. "The good receive miracles, and the evil...die."

This time the silence lasted a long time before Charmian walked to the large picture window overlooking the city and gazed down at the large crowds holding a candlelight vigil around St. Mary's on the other side of town.

"If what you say is true, Doctor LeCouer, what we have is an infallible process of healing. Incurables from all over the world will flock to St. Mary's and pay any price to be restored to good health."

LeCouer angrily responded, "Pay any price. My God, Charmian, you don't get it do you? These are miracles, not commercials for your MEDILARK medical circus."

Charmian was on fire with an idea. Nothing could stop her now. She moved in on her adversary to deliver a final blow.

"You're dead wrong, Doctor. Miracles are the highest form of commercials, reaching the widest audience with the most powerful sales pitch in the universe. The only difference between us and the city fathers at Fatima and Lourdes is that we're going to charge admission for our miracles, and that money will go into research to produce a whole lot more miracles."

The battle raged on all levels of society across the globe: who would decide who was a candidate for the Healing Room; What criteria would be used to determine what degree of goodness would be needed to insure a successful outcome; And, ultimately, what is goodness and who, if anybody, is qualified to make that judgment.

Charmian left these questions to the ethicists, theologians, philosophers, and judges to ponder and discuss. She quickly prepared the massive administration scheme to process the hundreds of thousands of requests that poured into NHE from the sick and dying of the world. She knew the hostile reaction from moralists would soon give way to the law of supply and demand, and today's heresy would become tomorrow's orthodoxy. After all, the same disruption rocked the medical world in the 1920's, when a London physician named Frederick Griffin tampered with the DNA structure of mice and opened to door to generic engineering, or when Baby Louise Brown was conceived in a lab dish in 1978. All met with startling opposition, but soon all quietly slipped into common practice. Charmian Kettering was an expert in product marketing. She knew the world was more interested in the goods and services of its technicians than the protestations of its philosophers. She knew the Healing Room would be no different. What she didn't know was how quickly the demand would override the opposition.

The first group of selectees were screened and ready for their medical rebirth within a week.

David LeCouer stood outside the now brightly lit St. Mary's. The venerable structure seemed to reel back from the attention like a proud, dying giant. He looked up to the fifth floor and the large neon white cross in the window. He looked up and down the street where a dozen network TV mobile trucks and their high tech paraphernalia had formed a complicated maze of antennas, cables, and satellite dishes that were blotting out the sun, while their chatty minions below were giving the world a blow-by-blow description of the latest miracle. Street vendors had staked out their turf to hark their wares: t-shirts, mugs, crosses, brochures, and a dozen varieties of plastic replicas of St. Mary's. The Christian Art League had already set up a kiosk and was doing a thriving business selling large day-glow posters of the hand of God piercing the San Francisco skyline, across the Golden Gate Bridge, through the low lying clouds, and gently caressing the fifth floor of the most famous hospital in the world. The inscription read:" San Francisco, the Chosen City. Home of The Healing Room."

The young doctor shook his head in sad disbelief. Like every other noticeable moment of our time, this one, perhaps the most significant, was being trans-formed into consumer entertainment, being hyped, groomed, retuned, reshaped into a media event, the ultimate reality show. Causes were lost; only effects and program ingredients were primary. No one would think for himself now or be touched by what might be the final warning for mankind. No, instead they would be electronically denuded, robbed of scope and personal meaning, as they sheepishly relinquished their wills again and assumed the only role they had been conditioned for—a silent viewer in the dark.

David was not a religious man, but he understood the miracles were not the message. They were only a framework, a spiritual metaphor, a cipher for the greater lesson in the mind of the Divinity that caused them.

He slowly walked back to his office and sat in the dark trying to make sense of things beyond the senses. He kept coming back to the obvious—goodness finds redemptive healing, and evil avoids the effort. People had to take sides now. The unscheduled cycle of spiritual warning was making its final appearance. Was that it? Was this the prelude to Armageddon promised by every prophet from St. John, the Evangelist, to Carl Sagan, the eminent star gazer? Was the Healing Room God's ultimatum to a world consumed with eroding the margins between good and evil and establishing the validity of moral chaos?

Dr. David LeCouer was an ethician. His job was to search for the essence of things and to decide the ennobling way for human behavior to proceed. He was proud of what he did, but now felt like the most useless man on the face of the earth. His lofty calling had lost its voice amid the deafening din of the Big Top Circus going up all around him. Was there some other way he could draw attention to the urgency of the message of the Healing Room, or was it even worth the bother? He stood at his window for hours feeling the inevitability of things. A hazy sun began to rise over the Bay Bridge, and he fell asleep at his desk.

MEDILARK never got past the model stage. The NME empire started crumpling soon after the Federal government indicted them on fourteen counts of billing fraud, sending their stock plummeting to an all time-low. The night before the Healing Room was scheduled to reopen, a massive fire of unknown origin engulfed St. Mary's and razed it to the ground. Two bodies were recovered. One was not identified, the other was that of Dr. David La Couer. It was never clear why the staff ethicist was in the empty building so late at night.

Speculation as to the cause of the blaze ran from a homeless person starting a fire to keep warm to arson and to Divine disgust.

Nothing was ever proven.

The following day, an editorial in the San Francisco Chronicle had a unique perspective:

> Perhaps mankind is unable to grasp the meaning of miracles, but it can surely understand the absence of them.
>
> The appearance of The Healing Room seemed to portend a greater possibility than restoring life to broken bodies. It dramatized man's ultimate choice between right and wrong and the hope there was still time for self-healing by committing to one and eradicating the other.
>
> That message was largely overshadowed while St. Mary's stood in the center of the commercial feeding furor that sought to devour the gift, but now, that only ashes remain, is the world waking to what really visited us on that magnificently shabby fifth floor on Stanyan Street?
>
> It seems all over the world the message of the Healing Room is being discussed in every newspaper, on every talk show, every mag-

azine article, and every public forum where thoughtful people gather.

Perhaps, sadly, it is only in loss that our species can ever appreciate the value of the gift. Perhaps, the fire that consumed St. Mary's was the final light needed to illuminate the lesson. In that respect, whoever or whatever initiated the blaze caused the greatest miracle of all.

The City Council unanimously voted to leave the ruins of St. Mary's as a lasting memorial, turning it into a peace and meditation park. They recanted two months later when a Salt Lake City based supermarket chain offered 30.8 million dollars to build an international food fair.

EVERYMAN'S
ULTIMATE DILEMMA

"Jesus Christ, how did this happen?"

Time and tide, that's how.

Tiny mounds of flesh appear all over your body without warning, mostly under the eyes and chin and along the neckline and, usually, at the same time ominous dark rings start circling the eye sockets.

Theo Pelakakis had reached his fifty-first birthday, and he didn't like what he saw staring back at him from the bathroom mirror.

He walked slowly into the tiny living room with the overflowing book shelves and mumbled to the big black-and-white portrait hanging over the faded brown leather couch, "Well, I beat you by ten years, Jack, but hell, is it worth it?" Theo was convinced he would die, like his literary hero, Jack London, at the height of his world renown, age forty-one.

He tried mightily to model his life on the same pathway as the legendary author/adventurer. He hadn't come close. Oh sure, there were moments of spontaneous brilliance that brought a few bites from the big time, but nothing ever came of it. So he plowed on with a manufactured hope he never really believed. Part-time community theater director, part-time freelance writer, and full time social studies teacher, all the while a stranger in a high-tech world he no longer understood or cared to.

He went back to the bathroom and turned off the light for the same reason a little kid diverts his fear by singing when he thinks there are monsters under the bed. He looked into the mirror again hoping his last impression was a fluke of that always uncomplimentary enemy of mirrors, direct white light. Reluctantly, he flicked the switch back on. No fluke. His time had come. He would have to contend with all those unwanted visitors other male fifty-plus diminishing mortals must face: thinning hair, ballooning breasts, a whole variety of "itis" maladies, and a growing obsession with his prostate gland that would cause him to devour megadoses of zinc and vitamin E all day.

He leaned closer to the mirror and slowly started moving his hands over his face like a blind man identifying the face of a stranger.

"It's all diet. All that crap I've been eating for thirty years. Hell, maybe I should have stayed married. At least I would have eaten right."

He didn't mean it. His first and only marriage lasted eleven months. When pushed for an explanation of why he never remarried, his eyes would narrow, and the muscles around his jaw would tighten pulling his mouth open like Indiana Jones trying to outrun an avalanche.

"Bottom line is I'm a loner; I need my space." Sometimes he'd add, "Some people just love their freedom more than their need for family."

That's what all dreamer's say who believe they're on a strict timetable with destiny and can't afford to slow the climb with other commitments. It's really all about fear, fear the dream will die without an exclusive solitary devotion. So, Theo dated many women, always as an afterthought, always for a short time. Play and move on. After all, he was a man on a mission bound for glory.

Attachments would only slow him down.

But now he was 51, his prospects were dead, and he had to think about these things. And he had three days to do it.

The Southwestern no-frills flight from Portland to Phoenix to San Antonio to Houston to New Orleans was filled with the same kind of people you find on commuter trains from the suburbs—lots of charcoal grays, a smattering of earth tones, and a few isolated blue-collar windbreakers, all jammed knees to chest in their space-saver seats, all chatty and clubby in superficial camaraderie. "I swear, these seats must have been designed by Tibetan monks," the tall thin black man with the plaid bow tie offered, trying to break the ice with his seat mate. No luck. Theo closed his eyes and his left brain was straining to lay out all the possible solutions to the most bone-rattling dilemma a 51-year-old bachelor can ever face—what kind of companionship do I choose for the few productive years I have left: comfort or lust?

Theo had long given up trying to find love, lust, and comfort in one mate, and had been carrying on simultaneous relationships at either end of the country for four years. Until now, he'd felt neither sordid nor duplicitous. As a matter of fact, he felt downright euphoric he had finally found the two primal satisfactions most men search for but never seem to find, with a clear conscience: warm comforting love and volcanic lust. The only problem was logistical, they resided in two different women, twenty-five hundred miles apart.

Cynnia Della Femina was comfort. She had known Theo since they first appeared in their grammar school play at St. Finbar's. Everything they were had a common bond—same neighborhood, same fear of the confessional, same old-fashioned values, same plucky sense of the absurd, same love of the performing arts. Cynnia was first cellist with the East Portland Philharmonic Orchestra, and, like Theo, had risen to the top of the minor leagues, but never got the call from the majors. She accepted it. Theo, of course, never could.

Yesterday she gave him a deadline. "I can't go on like this anymore, Theo. I love you with all my heart and you feel that love, but I just don't feel your love in return. I know, I know, you're a lone rider all wrapped up in your goals, but I need to know I'm loved. If you want me in your life, you need to let go and make a commitment; otherwise, let's end this halfhearted journey. Think about it, and call me Monday."

"Monday is good, Cynnia, I'll be coming back from a convention in New Orleans. Gives me time to think. I'll call Monday."

True, he would be coming back from New Orleans, but there was no convention. There was only the delicious anticipation of seeing the umpteenth reunion of the Firehouse Five Plus Five jazz immortals at Pete Fountain's joint and three days and four nights at the Maison St. Charles Quality Inn with…unbridled lust.

Sweet, southern widow, Betty Lujean Eccles was tintinnabulary passion, a willing explorer in any fantasy that pleased her man. A thirty-four year veteran of a sexless marriage, who now had an Olympian desire to reconstruct her atrophied libido. Both women were full-blown decent, valuable, caring companions who loved Theo, and he genuinely loved them, as best he understood love to be.

"God, I hate being 51."

It's hard to say whether Theo was thinking those words or actually speaking them, but the tall squirming black man still trying to get comfortable in his seat mumbled, "What was that?" Again, Theo ignored him.

The neckless gorilla at the front desk had already sweated through his white shirt and red tie and was pretty much through his maroon and beige gabardine uniform jacket. He didn't speak; he wheezed his words through a hacking cough that shook the five-tiered crystal chandelier overhead.

"Room 143, past the fountain and across from Miss Eberline's Praline Shoppe—eh, don't forget your TV remote."

"TV remote?", Theo repeated quizzically.

"Yeah, so many people were stealing them from the rooms, we have to issue them up front with the key. Hell, you can't trust anybody anymore. Know what I mean? Return it when you check out. Failure to do so will result in a fifty dollar charge being added to your credit card."

"I'll guard it with my life," Theo quipped, and then asked, "Is there a drugstore nearby? I need some aspirins."

The large clerk fighting a losing battle with the suffocating Louisiana humidity exhaled slowly and wheezed, "Yessah, a few blocks away, but we don't advise you walk around this neighborhood after dark. Not safe anymore, lots of muggings. For a slight service charge of five dollars, I could get the security guard to go for you just as soon as he gets back. He's checking a break-in on the fourth floor."

"No thanks. I just lost the headache. You think I'll make it to my room without getting shot?"

The big man ignored the humor and collapsed in an upholstered chair with a chandelier-shaking thud.

Betty Lujean wouldn't arrive from Atlanta via Atchawee, Tennessee, for another six hours. He had time to sort out his feelings, find the words, and choose to which lady he would declare a commitment.

He pulled all the curtains shut. He could think better in the dark, and it would be easier to talk out loud to his conscience, something he did a lot of lately.

"Why do I have to make a choice in the first place? Why can't I just go on seeing both, telling them each what they want to hear? No harm; no foul."

"Because you're 51, Theo, you can't afford the lie anymore. You rationalized it away before, because it didn't seem to hurt anyone and you were getting what you wanted. Now, it hurts. Besides, deep down you know it's unfair to two great ladies."

"Wouldn't it be a helluva lot more unfair to me to commit to one and be frustrated for the rest of my life? Don't I have a right to fulfill my needs for sex and love?"

"Sure you do, but you have no right to lie to get them. You've told each one of them you're not seeing other women. Stop being a player, Theo. Grow up and learn to be a committed lover."

"Ahuh, you're saying compromise. Commit to monogamy, then act like you're getting everything you need. That's the biggest lie of all, for crissakes. No, no, no!

Dammit, I can't do that. I want both. I need both. It's not my fault I can't find one woman who has it all."

"You want a mother in the kitchen and a whore in the bedroom, right?"

"Yes, yes, yes. Dammit, that's what every man wants deep down. We're just too damned religionized to tell the truth, too damned afraid admitting the need for animal lust makes us bad people, for crissakes, so we all pretend. We all settle for less. Antithesis becomes truth. The lie becomes fact. We mate and marry and bore ourselves to death with routine coupling and watch porn on the internet when the kids are sleeping."

"Everything becomes routine, Theo, but a routine of fantastic love lasts a lot longer than a routine of fantastic sex and fantasy. So if you have to choose between routines, choose love, pal."

He's not aware he's shouting at the top of his lung power.

"TO HELL WITH CIVILITY! I'M A PRIMORDIAL BEAST. LOVE IS NOT ENOUGH. I NEED TO CLIMB MOUNT EROS. MY GOD, HOW MUCH TIME DO I HAVE LEFT? I WANT UNCENSORED GIRLS GONE WILD, DELICIOUS ATOMIC LUST. THAT'S MY CHOICE. FINIS. PERIOD. END OF DEBATE." He let out a Tarzan yell accompanied with the appropriate chest pounding. The knock at the door was just as intense.

"Security here. Are you all right in there?"

Without pausing, Theo replied, "I'm fine. Just a little mid-life crisis. Everything's under control, officer. How's the break-in investigation going?"

Betty Lujean arrives—textile plant line foreman, a consistent 200 bowler, grandmother, and six times a year in different motels across the country, a brazen vixen, a shameless hussy, a Sheharazard, a Salome, A Mamie Stover without portfolio but with all the moves. She has found a man she feels safe with exploring the limits of human sexuality with occasional side trips to mythical sex. She wants to please and carries a separate silver metal suitcase of love inducements that would melt the heart of a warrior pope.

Theo hung out the "Do Not Disturb "sign and climbed Mount Eros most of the afternoon and early evening. They laughed and rode the St.Charles street car into the French Quarter, where they watched the endless parade of gawking pleasure seekers dutifully playing the parts of sophisticated bon vivants on holiday. They pretended they enjoyed having the roofs of their mouths burned bayou black from the super spicy gumbo soup at the historic Court of the Two Sisters. They continued their harmless pretense and "sucked da' head and pinchin' da tail" of red hot Cajun crawfish and all its accompanying rich delicacies, and topped off their tourist roles with a nighttime dinner/jazz cruise aboard the venerable steamboat, Natchez, where they hugged a lot in the half-moonlight. But, for Theo, it was all prelude, the dance before the feast. Oh, he did it well, all those simple, everyday things in a relationship like listening, asking her how she felt about things, holding hands, and never interrupting quiet moments, but he was never quite sure he was acting a part or genuinely involved. What he did know was that he was always looking forward to the end of day, a darkened room, a sliver of moonbeam, soft music, and the slow erotic rituals of mating.

Tonight, their second night, Betty Lujean would do what she always did on their second night. She would sense it was "that time," pick up her silver metal suitcase, walk into the bathroom, and emerge a few minutes later in the slinky black dress Theo sent her a week after they met on the YMCA discounted cruise to six Latin American countries. She would transform herself into everyman's fantasy moving seductively back into the darkened room, sit cross-legged in front of him, and begin a sensuous exploration of her body that never failed to excite a firestorm of possibilities.

Theo would do what he always did—sit on the couch, close his eyes, take deep breaths, lock away his guilt and dissatisfactions of being a man without a quest anymore, and savor the heart-pounding anticipation of melding with the most exotic playmate he could ever imagine.

He had reached the one secret place every man so desperately desired. His wish, however ineptly expressed, was her willing command.

He lit the scented candles, put on The Best of Julio Inglesias in his handheld cassette, and opened the curtains just far enough to allow a few square feet of the Louisiana harvest moon to create a touch of magic. He sat down on the ante bellum green velvet couch with the white and pink magnolia blossoms and closed his eyes.

Something was wrong. What? It was his conscience again, dammit.

"Whatdahell are you doing here? Beat it, leave me be. I've made my decision."

"Theo, when this thing is over, what will you be left with? What's going to fill the in-between times? You're using this woman for your own physical gratification, no more. You have nothing else to give her. You're flying under false colors. That's wrong...wrong...wrong."

The little voice trailed off.

He opened his eyes. Betty Lujean was standing in front of him, but no clingy black see-thru dress, no slow erotic moves, no fires burning. Instead she was wearing the same red and white Atlanta Braves tee shirt and black Bermuda shorts she had on when she slinked into the bathroom.

"Theo, I'm so nervous. I don't know where to start." She was clutching her hands the way church ladies do when they have to tell the pastor they need more money for altar flowers.

"Start anywhere, honey. You know we can talk about anything."

The farm lady from central Tennessee talked a long, long time, but Theo didn't hear much of it after she said she needed more from their relationship than just wonderful lovemaking. He suddenly went deaf, most feeling left his body, and he could only sense the movement of his eyes as they slowly scanned the room, picking out those inconsequential things he'd never seem to have noticed before. There was the hairpin on the floor behind the curled-up telephone cord by the bed, the changing shadows that crept through the venetian blinds on the side window, the way a simple, honest farm lady wrestling with deep emotion moves her big toes inside her shoes before speaking.

The return flight to Portland was less than half-filled. Theo sat in the back, all alone.

He needed to think about his losses. No more flights of fantasy six times a year. No more Jekyll and Hyde. No more pretending. The thrill of polygamy was gone, so was his great dilemma. Now, at least, he could call Cynnia and commit to her with a clear conscience.

"So what if those secret carnal lusts would never again be satisfied? So what if those little urgings that push all men to the border of delectable danger would have to be fought back time and time again? Hell, it's part of the male DNA. All men do it every time they step back and look at the flatness of their everyday lives.

Commitment for a man is a compromise, and that's the price he pays for decency, period. Besides, Cynnia is a good woman who loves me."

He was probably speaking above a mumble, because the chubby little kid three rows ahead of him with the crew cut and mustard stains on his Batman tee shirt was staring.

Theo looked at him with nothing in his eyes and reached for a thought slowly dawning, "Choosing the masquerade of a decent life, I guess that's what being 51 is all about, kid. Accepting compromise...on everything."

Theo did what he always did when he came home to his little cottage at the other end of the park. He put on some hot water for tea, pressed the big black message button on his answering machine, and looked for the moon. It was hanging just outside his kitchen window. It was one of those "maybe it's full or maybe it's seven-eights, I really can tell" moons.

The messages droned on—a neighborhood watch meeting, two wrong numbers, an automated sales pitch for Good Housekeeping Magazine, and then the soft, melodic rhythms of a familiar voice, "Theo, I've been thinking. It was very wrong of me to give you an ultimatum, when I knew all along you were giving me all you could give. It should be my decision, not yours. I love you but need and want more in return, and you can't give it to me. It's nobody's fault. It's just the way it is. You are a loner, Theo, and I guess you're really happier that way. Be good to yourself, and—goodbye."

He stood in the middle of his living room with the overcrowded book shelves for a long time waiting for something. He wasn't quite sure what. Nothing arrived. Then he began to look at inconsequential things he'd never quite noticed before like the perfect symmetry of a spider's web on the bottom shelf, the stubby butcher's pencil in Jack London's hand in the large portrait, and the way everything seems to lose its color and become something else when you suddenly feel alone.

Finally, he pulled out a stack of his seventy-eight records and put three Harry James and one Billie Holiday on the turntable.

He pulled the kitchen window curtains as far apart as they would go, sat in his big brown recliner chair under the framed autographed picture of the 1948 New York Yankees, and watched the moon.

It wasn't long before he quietly assessed, "Definitely seven-eights— or maybe not."

THE PLAZA OF OLD
MEN

He'd reached the age when small things don't matter anymore. The food stains on his faded olive drab shirt, the frayed dungarees, the black leather sandals worn through at the heels, the long hours sitting motionless in direct sunlight were of no consequence to his world. Like the dozens of other old men in the Plaza de Armas in Old San Juan, he had come to the end of things, and there was nothing left but to sit in the square.

They were everywhere—sitting on benches, on the steps of the ancient bandstand, on the rim of the crumbling water fountain with its stone carved statues of huddled saints and Greek deities, on the broken curb in front of the pharmacia at the northeast corner. Old men in brown shoes with broom handled canes, neatly trimmed mustaches, looking, waiting, seeing things young men have no time for, stoic, patient, willing to let the day come to them, watching simple things as if each were a miracle slowly unfolding for the first time—a child eating ice cream, bumper to bumper open air tour buses clogging the Calle de la Fortaleza with their gawking, chatty occupants, dark-skinned old ladies balancing bulging baskets of clothes on their heads, dogs sleeping in the midst of scavenging pigeons, bums honing in on trash cans quick to pounce on likely prospects, the potbellied cop in the two shades of dirt brown uniform with red socks openly taking bribes allowing motorists to park under the *No Parking* signs ringing the square.

Time passes, the sun shifts in the clear silver blue Puerto Rican sky, and on cue, the old men rise under some primordial command, and move in precise cadence from one bench to another, following the shade, a slow motion parade of ancients with nothing left to do but wait. They repeat their ritual of passage several times during the day—all but one.

El Viejo in the fading olive drab shirt with the tiny Cuban flag pinned to his torn breast pocket remains on the stone slab sticking through the broken sidewalk in front of the bandstand. In the simple unscripted play unfolding in this place, he is obviously a separatist, shunned by the others. Isolated. Outcast. But why?

The intense August heat intrudes every pore, stifling any sustained movement, but El Viejo shows no signs of discomfort. What makes him so immune to pain? Is it some mystical inner discipline, or just a simple preoccupation with other thoughts?

He sits undisturbed, bent, still clinging to the familiar peasant's pride in survival. Like the rest, he has nothing much to look forward to, but there is something else. He knows something that gives the monotony a purpose.

I watched this strange stationary endurance for five days. Finally, I broke the unwritten code of the plaza and spoke to El Viejo.

"Good morning, sir, nice day."

I have no way of knowing if my words entered his consciousness. His deeply lined face showed no sign of recognition. His black ivory eyes continued to scan the square in the same slow, predictable sweep as before. I sat next to him until the sun left the plaza and the vendors had packed their hand carved maracas, genuine imitation leather goods, and a thousand other gaudy tourist reminders of a Caribbean holiday and departed. We watched the end of day in silence.

I'm not sure why I was fascinated by El Viejo. Maybe it was that quiet dignity and control that universally attracts all seekers, that unforced contentment some old men have at the end of their lives that helps younger men shed the fear of entering their own final chapter. Maybe that, or just the need to know the reason the rest of his brotherhood had placed him in unconditional exile.

On my last day on the island, I continued my vigil watching the old men of the plaza, wondering about their stories, stories they freely and continuously exchanged. There was the old man in the shiny black suit, hawking secondhand tool kits to uninterested tourists, who claimed to be a personal confidante of Ernest Hemingway, although there's no proof the venturesome writer ever visited the island; the dark mahogany unshaven chap in the plaid trousers and green jacket who pointed with great pride to pictures in a yellowing scrapbook of a colorfully ruffled rumba dancer in a triumphant bow on a large outdoor stage; the man who fathered twenty-one children, but could only remember the names of four; another who cried a lot while producing old love letters from Puerto Rico's most famous national poetess, Julia de Burgos, insisting he was the inspiration for all her acclaim. "Sadly she went to New York, died on the street, and was buried as an 'unknown person.' If she had only listened to me." There was the small man with the oversized glass eye who insisted he was the one who created the motto for his country, "Bread, Land and Liberty," while working as the personal secretary to Luis Munoz Martin, the founder of the National Democratic Party.

You can never be sure in a place like this if people are who they say they are. It may make little difference. Truths are, perhaps, treacherous wraiths that often change color as the light of history falls at seasonal angles. So in the end nothing is clear but the single thought everything you've been doing all your life is no longer relevant; only the story that survives matters.

I asked the man in the shiny black suit about El Viejo. His eyes narrowed, he bent over and whispered, "Old fool. Thinks he fought with Castro in the Sierra Maestra. He's never left the island, the old fool."

As the well-dressed tourists from the posh Hotel Central on the southeast corner started trickling out for a night on the town, I bought a bottle of water from the kiosk refreshment stand and walked over to El Viejo. I sat for a moment and then handed him the frosted bottle. To my very great surprise, he looked up, made eye contact, and extended his gnarled weather-beaten hand and gently, almost ceremoniously, took it from me. A slight smile started forming in the deep valleys of his sun-baked cheeks and slowly made its way across the broad angles of a face chiseled in pock-marked granite. He raised the bottle to his scorched forehead to a point above a large winding scar and pressed it to his skin. He rolled it from one side to another, smiled again, offered a barely audible "gracias, senor," and handed the unopened bottle back to me.

Was he really a Fidelista, a Barbudo, one of the legendary bearded men of the mountains who carried squirrel rifles and helped bring down the most oppressive dictatorship in the hemisphere?

How well did he know Fidel, one of the most riveting personalities of the twentieth century? What does he know that history doesn't know? Why did he leave Cuba? Why is he now alone? I wanted to ask all of these things, but I didn't. The stories of the plaza served best, it seemed, if left undisturbed.

I don't know how long we sat in easy silence watching the life in the square, but the evening shadows were gone and some of the well-dressed tourists were returning to the Hotel Central when El Viejo pushed himself forward, stood up, and looked down Calle de San Jose with the same resigned uncertainty a sailor watches an oncoming storm. It was a deeply angled street twisting downward over jutting cobblestones and gaping sink holes, rising from the darkness toward the waterfront and a small park, where another group of old men played dominoes under dimly lit street lamps.

For the endless stream of young people walking up and down, it was a routine passage, not for El Viejo. It would be an agonizing challenge for an old man who had lost the assurance of his steps.

Suddenly, years of pain disappeared. He stood ramrod straight and made brisk, sweeping attempts to smooth his rumpled shirt the way soldiers do before an inspection. He turned to me with a voice that was no longer old and uncertain and declared, "You know, senor, I fought with Fidel."

I watched him as he became old again and inched his way down past a hundred obstacles and disappeared into the park.

Curiosity drove me to scan dozens of books and hundreds of magazine articles on the revolution that held the world spellbound in the late fifties when three hundred ill-equipped farmers defeated a brutalizing modern army of fifty thousand with sheer willpower and the ability to hit hard and run fast.

My big magnifying glass moved over the ruddy, bearded faces of just about every published picture of Fidel's famous ragtag band of peasant rebels without recognizing the one face I was searching for.

Then a new book by syndicated journalist, Georgie Anne Geyer—*Guerilla Prince, The Untold Story of Fidel Castro*—appeared on the scene. There it was on page 207, a picture of nine tired, scruffy somber-faced men in the familiar sweat-stained, rumpled olive drab uniforms of the Sierra Maestra heroes. The caption read, *"These were the legendary 'men of the mountains' only days after they marched on Havana, strange but victorious warriors of our time."*

My magnifying glass stopped on the intense, thin warrior kneeling in the forefront. He held a World War I carbine in big, gnarled, weather-beaten hands. A large winding scar on his forehead was barely visible through the first stage of a noticeable grin. A tiny Cuban flag was pinned to his cartridge belt crisscrossing his chest.

Perhaps, time had not stolen truth from at least one story in the plaza of old men.

YARD WORK

Old age and death made no sense to her at all, but gardening did.

She had given up her highly awarded renowned search for universal answers twenty-three years ago and replaced it with perennials, seedlings, and silver bags of Miracle Mulch. At age eighty-three, she moved with the quiet assurance of a retired Arctic explorer who had unraveled all the mysteries worth knowing.

Everything else was gone: the TV, the family pictures, the white lace doilies, the three boxes of 8mm movies of trips, parties, backyard barbeques, holidays, candid surprises, and all the other family trivia that seemed so monumental at the time.

"Hell, there just isn't any possibility in memories anymore," she quietly muttered with no sign of rancor or regret.

In less than twenty-four hours, with the help of Goodwill, the Salvation Army, and a day laborer named Ernesto, her settled life of hostile boredom was gone.

Furniture, paintings, cars, dishes, unopened boxes of stuff, even the old brown leather address book with all the red lines through most of the names and the word "deceased" scratched over them. Without regard for legacy, sentimentality or economics, the contents of a life of well-ordered clutter were unceremoniously loaded into large, gray trucks, which rumbled off to storefront distribution centers to be recycled back into other lives of clutter with no regard for their history.

This final irreverence for a life's collectibles delighted her.

She laughed at the emptiness, even sang a few lines of *Wait Til The Sun Shines, Nellie*, just to hear the echo bouncing off the bare walls and rugless mahogany floors. She laughed again, listening to the sound of fun rustling in the back of her throat. She was twelve years old again, rolling down the sand dunes of the Hamptons, eyes shut tight, giggling as only a young girl on the edge of naughtiness can, flailing her arms to catch every twist and turn of the biting ripples of collapsing sand beneath her. It was something proper young ladies in white satin dresses didn't do, and that made the illogic of real life even sweeter. It was a simple, joyous impulse common to all childhoods, but it remained alive and present in all her daydreams, easily retrieved and immediately nourishing for reasons she never bothered to examine. She could see herself coming to rest at the bottom of Pirates Peak, the highest promontory on the three-mile stretch of primordial shoreline. She'd lain there for about a thousand years it seemed, wondrously mesmerized by the rolling, billowing clouds above, dancing wildly to the fickle rhythms of celestial physics, creating and recreating nature's most fascinating murals in motion. White fluffy Teddy bears appeared and just as quickly turned into stern-faced eagles in slow motion flight, which soon gave way to a hundred more silky transitions that only a child's imagination can readily identify.

She had never looked at clouds before, no time, really. There was private school, all that meaningless Latin and Greek homework the nuns delighted in requiring, ballet class, trips to the museums, memorized recitations from poetry so foreign to common sense she had no idea what words to emphasize for dramatic effect, so she emphasized them all.

"Daddy said I sounded like a muleskinner shouting at ornery animals who wouldn't budge," she said to no one in particular as she walked through the empty two-room cottage on her way to the dark blue shed standing sentinel behind the rear entrance.

"You want to be a great poet? Create images so damn obscure even you have no idea what the hell they mean. That's the answer, believe me. Forget meter and rhyme, boys and girls, go for obscurity. They'll name libraries and stretches of highway after you."

She got no response from the hand forks, swan-necked hoes, pitch-forks and other neatly placed tools of the earth overcrowded into the four-by-eight metal room.

With surgical deftness, she eased her crippled hands into the red cloth gardening gloves with the rubber reinforced finger tips. Her casual monologue continued as she bent down to put on the big bulky knee pads.

"You remember when every basketball player used to wear knee pads like this? Seemed eminently reasonable. Big bodies under a full head of steam bumping in to one another bone to bone, falling to the floor, being crushed by bigger bodies. Same physical danger today, but no knee pads. Form has replaced function, that's why. Fashion, not reason, is the new god, and the hell with them all."

She filled her rolling cart with three small digging tools, an oil glistening serrated hand saw and a brand new device with the red, white, and blue label shouting "Super Weeder" through the unwrapped cellophane.

She grabbed it firmly and held it up to the dusky light with the sneering arrogance of a Comanche admiring a prized scalp.

"Ahhh, now I've got 'ya. Let the battle begin, me hardies"

She placed two sets of large iron hand cutters on the bottom shelf of the cart.

Today's strategy was to attack the invading oleander bushes ringing her fence, cascading backward with twelve-foot high three-inch thick stalks threatening to engulf the property in an eerie gothic canopy like angry jungle underbrush reclaiming one of those lost Mayan cities.

She'd carefully scan the enemy stalks for a cutting target, a soft spot that might give more willingly as she clamped down with the heavy duty iron cutters. She knew that was a futile search. Oleander in full bloom is as difficult to split as a crowbar right from the blast furnace, but it was the game she played on her subconscious.

"If my brain thinks it's going to be an effortless venture, then it won't tell my body to contort in pain every time I use every ounce of strength in my limbs to squeeze the handles together and pray for a cut before the veins in my forehead explode all over the front yard. I can see the obituary now, 'Pulitzer Prize winning local poetess and yard work enthusiast, Mary Maynard Kaynes, lost a battle with her oleander today and died instantly from pruning shock.'"

Her laughter fooled her body again as a mighty oleander stalk split in half and uneventfully fell to the ground. Soon a thirty-yard swath of straight line cutting had thinned out the relentless poisonous evergreen shrub and opened large windows in the fenceline inviting sunshine to filter through and work its magic on the summer mums and snowball marigolds nearby. Sherman's march through Georgia could not have been more lethally efficient as the old lady with laughing determination cut, whacked, and disposed of the unwanted overgrowth, unabated except for occasional pauses for large delightfully sloppy swigs of water from a two-gallon bottle still wearing a Carcinelli's Dago Red Wine label. Sometimes she'd just pour the contents over her head and stand perfectly still seemingly aware of every bead of sweat on her body being neutralized by the cooling visitor. She reveled in silence like an Olympic athlete taking a shower after recording her best time ever.

Her deepest breath of the afternoon ended with, "Ah, the best part of the day."

It was a lie. The real soul-rattling highpoint of her day was moments away in the person of a pleasant walking antiquity wearing a simple light green cotton dress, smartly accented by the town's last remaining hat with a functioning veil.

The old lady carefully removed her left glove to check the time on the happy face watch she wore as her only concession to sentimentality. She had promised her first great-grandchild she would wear it "until the cows came home," and she never broke a promise in her life. It was 5:05, and that meant a daily ritual that was as predictable as her 3:30 walk to the little blue shed and one she secretly looked forward to the way young artists look forward to their first public showing.

Ms. Elvina Bascomb Reed, the secretary-treasurer of the local Literary Society and chief librarian of the Mary Maynard Kaynes library rounded the northeast corner of the old lady's property line on her usual mile-and-half walk home from work. One would imagine the state's most valued expert on every aspect of the old lady's life in literature, a dogged curator who had read and reread all 2,243 poems, 872 magazine and newspaper articles, 16 books and every public statement ever uttered on the planet about her subject, would delight in their routine meetings. One would imagine, but one would be wrong. The two ironclad independent octogenarians had everything in common but speech. It had nothing to do with the mysteries of female conflict. Economy in conversation was a religion in this part of the northeast, and motives were seldom questioned. People, mostly old people, did what they did and were given a free pass of placid acceptance for any behavior short of murder and voting Republican. No one really knew if it was a holdover from a rigid Calvinist past, or simply because most folks up here had very little to say about anything. The unremarkable scene proceeded as it had for two decades.

"Why Ms. Kaynes, you have the most beautifully landscaped yard in this county; it is a gift to Mother Nature herself."

No eye contact. No greeting. No acknowledgement that the other was breathing the same air less than seven feet away.

The librarian never seemed to care if her words were heard, and the poetess was certain the librarian never saw her guarded smile of pride as she turned away.

On and on she went. Low leaning ten foot branches of crepe myrtle and golden rain trees dutifully fell like proud General officers before a conquering enemy's firing squad. Gardenia, summersweet and rose-of-Sharon shrubs were smartly and geometrically cut back, cut down, reshaped, or thinned out in perfect symmetry.

As usual, sharp pin pricks of pain shot up and down her suntanned sinewy arms, as the small of her back compressed inward like a jaw reacting to a knockout blow. But mind over matter always worked for her every time the shadows washed over her otherwise routine life. The pain continued, but without any power to influence her whacking, cutting, sawing, chopping and stacking.

The old lady laughed and hummed and laughed again. Gratification was instant and success dramatically evident as the piles of cuttings ignored the haphazard throwing into the center of the yard and had mystically formed a striking five-foot pyramid just as clear and meticulous in design as if planned by the Pharaoh's architect—well, almost.

She was a poet. Symbols, real or imagined, never escaped her comment.

"Will you look at that," she exclaimed. "I've climbed the temples of Chichen-Itza and Tulum, slogged through three miles of that God awful Peruvian red mud to sit on top of Machu Picchu for days listening for ancient whispers. Nothing. Not a syllable. But you," pointing to the unintentional home grown pyramid of garden waste, "you can't stop talking." And she listened, occasionally shaking her head in easy agreement to the leafy monologue only she could hear.

With the help of Mr. Carcinelli's big bottle, she again treated herself to another marathon winner's crossing-the-finishing-line shower. Suddenly the pin pricks became thunderbolts, and her left arm went limp, hanging uselessly at her side like tinsel on a discarded Christmas tree. With her right hand pressed firmly against the crease in the dangling assaulted limb, she looked down at it and shouted, carefully emphasizing every word.

"No, dammit. I won't have it, you understand. Go away, you're not wanted here. Go away, now. You hear me, now."

She repeated the spirited mantra again and again. Then, the rubber-tipped fingers on the left hand began to move, slowly at first but gaining more animation as she raised the arm and shook it like a ball-player shaking off an injury. Once more her body complied.

"Okay, boys and girls, we're back in the saddle." She eyed the red, white, and blue cellophane package on her moving cart the way a home run hitter eyes a fastball heading straight for his wheelhouse.

"Let the battle begin."

The spongy kneepads gave just enough under her weight to pamper the arthritis raging in ever joint of her body, as she knelt in the narrow pathway between the early purple orchids and the veteran white primrose.

She took out the Super Weeder hand tool, beaming with delight as if she had just discovered fire, and began the doomed crusade the world of gardening fights with more and more technology, predestined to win small skirmishes but never a final victory.

Of all her work hours, weeding, the most fruitless drudgery, gave her the greatest pleasure. She had outlived the need to question why.

When her two husbands died suddenly and left her with demanding creditors, when the flash floods tore her cottage from its foundations and washed away half her home and three hundred unpublished poems being readied for her last anthology, she found all the therapy she needed in the soil, ridding her beloved eight-tenths of an acre of relentless invaders.

"Why haven't you written a single line of poetry in twenty-three years?" "Which of your poems best describes your personal philosophy?" "For a society so desperately in search of higher meaning, why is there so little modern poetry?"

Badgered by the local media, who bi-annually knocked on her door digging for a new angle to unlock the enigma of the area's only bona fide celebrity since Ethan Allen and his Green Mountain Boys bivouacked on a hill two miles outside of town in the winter of 1775, she gave her standard response:

"In eighty years of plucking rhyme and meter out of my imagination I've come to the conclusion the best we can do to make sense out of mysteries is right out there".

Pointing to her garden, "It's our relationship to serving the primal needs of the earth that clarifies our purpose. It's all out there. You want meaning, go prune a bush. Give the plant a chance to grow strong, remove all excess from living things, carry off the dead leaves, remember to lift with your knees, never your back, but most importantly, find a way to stay ahead of your weeds."

She particularly enjoyed making the next point raising her voice to near shouting while emphasizing every word, "Lay bare the earth in your garden, then take a vacation for a few months. When you come back, what will you see?" She never waited for a response. "Weeds. Why? Because the natural condition of the universe is for weeds. Negativity has first priority in the world of vegetation. It is both the constant burden and highest calling of we alien humans to fight for the flowers. All the poetry that ever was doesn't add up to more enlightenment than a good hard day of yard work. Now, if you don't mind, you'll have to leave. I'm an old lady, and I get bored very easily." Her consistent soliloquy soon led many to add the word *eccentric* before mentioning her name.

An unusually warm winter led to an early spring. That meant an earlier start for gardeners, farmers, and other cultivators of the earth to begin a new cycle of life, selecting suitable locations for planting out crops in the fields and new annuals in the flower beds, checking light exposure, drainage, and fertility, then preparing the soil.

Time and seasons had no effect on the old lady. She instinctively felt the rhythms of the earth and adapted to its new urgencies without missing a beat in her four hours a day, seven day a week labor in the fading sun.

But there were differences. The sharp pin pricks of pain came more often, leaving her left arm hanging uselessly at her side. Her slurred speech, too inaudible now to shout down the maladies spreading out of control, robbed her iron will of its greatest ally.

Like a proud gladiator ignoring wounds to continue the fight, she pushed her cart south past the trellised gazebo toward the blazing red-and-orange satiny lupines standing ramrod straight alongside the genteel bowing mariposa lilies.

She thought she saw a patch of nut grass creeping into the bed. Just as she reached for the Super Weeder, a new pain, more intense than the others exploded inside her chest. She fell to the ground amid the rich colors of a dozen blooming annuals, slowly sprawling out on the soft bed of flowers like a child making a snow angel in the sand. For a moment, her body was young again, inhaling deeply the way you do when you search to retrieve an elusive scent. A soft smile erased the wrinkles in her golden brown, weather-beaten face as she counted the teddy bears and slow moving birds in the clouds and breathed in the salt-tipped richness of a faraway shoreline.

The most famous resident of the northeast corner of the state was laid to rest in the Fair Oaks Cemetery on a hill overlooking the Ethan Allen Botanical Gardens.

Ms. Elvina Bascomb Reed was asked to search her unquestioned expertise and find the economical sentiment that would best synopsize the celebrated poetess' rhythmic genius for making sense of both our beauty and our travail.

The simple headstone continues to confound out-of-state visitors to this day.

Mary Maynard Kaynes
Poet Laureat of New Hampshire
1917–2000
"Tend to your garden.
Weeds Happen"

SEARCHING FOR
HULA LOVE UNDER
A BLUE PAPAYA
MOON

The adventure of a lifetime was about to begin. The fate of the species was the grand prize.

He sat on the crumpling stone seawall like a condemned man waiting for a last minute reprieve staring at the giant millennium clock over the harbor master's office…247 Hours 46 Minutes 35 Seconds. He had exhausted all his possibilities. He knew his life depended upon movement. He just didn't know where to go.

Across the street, Old Martinique was parading up and down rue de Liberte with its brightest Caribbean colors hawking tourist trash for the passengers of the big white boat in the bay.

Their plastered smiles did little to conceal their lazy disdain for anything commercial. These pitch black descendants of slaves from the festering holes of sixteenth century West Indies trade ships were made for eatin', laughin', makin' babies, and singin' in the shade, not selling seashell necklaces, Creole Lady pin cushions and Don't Worry, Be

Happy t-shirts. They had no choice. They didn't own their island, and never would. They were children who needed the benediction of the invader—first the French, then the English, and now the French again, with strong support from the Indian merchants monopolizing the trendy shops facing the sea. A new age of conscious evolution was about to begin. The planet again was at that point of decision, move this way and redeem the promise or move that way and write the final chapter. The species now had all the tools to reinvent itself in whatever image it so choose, but time was on the side of the Dark Forces. The sun was about to complete its life cycle and burn all the planets making us all star children, a new galactic species. Memories of earthbound life would have to be reconstructed by new forms trying to piece together the origin of life on Earth, a self-deluding empyrean realm of the elite.

Every age has its ordained mutant warriors who combine the past with a vision of the future and then go ahead and create it. Lucifer with his apple in the Garden of Eden, Eric, the Red with his long ships, Moliere, his satires, Nobel, his gunpowder, and now in the final moments of the old century, probably Prigogene and his Second Law of Thermodynamics explaining how the laws of nature change at higher levels of complexity. Everything had gotten about as complex as was possible at the end of this one hundred. The next one hundred, if there were to be a next one hundred, was up for grabs. The Mindbogglers had misread the stars as usual and placed all hope with the Human Genome Marchers and the Dotcom Acro Dancers with their dream of uniting the world with a one stop, one shop, all purpose credit card. But Unitas, tired of its fifteen-million year journey of transformation had placed the E-link cipher into one sixty-plus, slightly overweight seawall sitter in washed gabardines and mismatched socks.

Of course, he had no idea he, alone, had the power to make the decision that would end social chaos and overwhelming human degradation. It probably would have made no difference if he did. He was nearing the end of his life where all concerns are obsessively self-centered, particularly when a lingering case of hemorrhoids resists all attempts at relief. All he knew was that everything good and meaningful was fading in his life with every passing second on the biggest digital sign in the eastern Caribbean.

Oh sure, he had tried to forget the past and adapt. Right after he received his penile implant, he changed his name from Molyneaux Kepplewaithe to Bombay Curry. He started to wear his baseball cap backwards, got in the habit of saying, "wassup?" and misplacing his modifiers until his English was totally unrecognizable. He bought a laptop, went on line, and soon started adding a new name to his Buddy List every day. He even hosted his own chat room and had a virtual orgasm with a widow in Salt Lake City named Hotflashes@ AOL. com, but nothing worked. Like all the other over-sixties of his profile group, he began to see everything as a coming attraction for the Apocalypse—car stereos, daytime TV, alternate lifestyles, Court TV, and everyday stuff like that.

But he refused to see himself as a victim. He was grounded in the values of the century that was about to end, and he would not give up. He understood that if life gave us all the answers, we'd lose our freedom. He knew the ambiguity of the world was what kept hope alive. So he did what his generation did best. He persisted, and it paid off, sorta.

One night he fell asleep in his imitation brown leather reclining chair after watching an American Movie Classics retrospective on Sonny Tuffs. When he awoke, he heard a voice. It happens a lot when you're over sixty. He wasn't sure where it came from, memory, conscience, or just one of those unexplainable and unattached commands that bypass your will and demand action like sneaking downstairs on Christmas Eve and opening one of your presents when no one is around. When you're over sixty you know these voices are always a combination of people and events that walked in and out of your life sometime in the past, maybe unnoticed. You really have no choice but to listen and act and let the consequences be damned. This was one of those voices. It was loud, clear and urgent. "Find Hula Love." There was a problem. He had no idea who or what she or it was.

He accepted the message. Why not? He was a simple come-as-you-are guy who understood what all simple life understands. We're all conclusions of our own history. If you can't accept that, what's the point of standing upright anymore? His past was telling him Hula Love alone had the answers. If he could find it, things would change and mortality would make sense. He could be certain again that the nurturing myths and ideals of his childhood in the lost world would soon be replaced by a new understanding of what the world could be. After all, he was homo sapiens. He had no choice but to believe the future would be better. He didn't know how or why he knew this but he had the old reliable default, faith. And faith had preordained everything in his life.

His mother had always told him, "You know more about baseball than anyone in the whole wide world." And mom was made of steel and mortar and saw things and knew stuff that no other mortal in his town would ever understand. He believed her, and became the youngest chief of umpires in the history of the Eastern Iowa Cornfield Class AA League until his right index finger was hit by lightening in a playoff game and forced him into early retirement. Didn't Monsignor Phiffenlufer tell him God would punish him when he discovered him and another altar boy in an awkward tandem masturbation experiment before a funeral mass for Sister Mary George? He believed the solemn man in red and black robes who bought a new Cadillac every year and drank more wine at mass than all the other priests combined and understood his inability to get another erection until the day he visited a Tijuana whorehouse to celebrate his twenty-seventh birthday was simple Divine retribution, no more.

A silver metal sky was pushing down on tight clusters of cotton ball clouds racing toward the Pacific, when he again met up with the Kahuna Lady. A light, warm rain, more refreshing than annoying, was falling over the western rim of the Halemaumau crater of the Kilauea volcano. Bombay stopped and moved both sides of his face into the wind to catch the full measure of the rain. It reminded him of his Navy days on a sleek ship of the line plowing through angry seas spraying thick sheets of water back over the weather decks. He'd always felt that was the only real true adventure in life, and he never missed an opportunity to relive it. He had faith the old Kahuna Lady in the red lava glow muu muu and the fresh hibiscus in her hair was telling him the truth: that his life, any life would be unfulfilled until he listened to the voice and found Hula Love. Didn't she cure the cancer inside his large intestine with that smelly concoction of dried plumeria leaves, burnt pine needles, and filtered red dirt from the rim of the crater? Didn't she put him on an eleven-day fast of rain water and Lilikoi pits ten years earlier during his mid-life crisis? Sure he lost twenty-eight pounds and swallowed four teeth biting into the granite center of the yellow pits, but life after fifty did fill with meaning, at least until now. He was banking on her history to push him through this final home-stretch where nothing was clear and nothing was working anywhere.

After all, he was homo sapiens, and he had to make sense out of chaos and regain his heart.

"Where do I find Hula Love?" he asked her as she wrapped a gray-black petrified rock in a giant T-leaf as an offering to the fire goddess, Madam Pele.

The old Kahuna Lady never spoke above a whisper, her words flowed effortlessly like moon shadows sliding over a meadow.

"Never mistake movement for meaning, but keep moving forward. Listen for the voice within and drink twenty-two glasses of water a day."

"Twenty-two? I thought ten was the recommended daily allowance."

"Most problems in life," she said, "are caused by fatigue and boredom. Most fatigue is caused by dehydration, and all boredom is caused by not getting up and moving to another place."

"Yeah, okay, but twenty-two glasses a day?"

"Remember, fertile crops are so because the irrigation ditch is never empty."

He had no idea what the hell that meant, but the Kahuna Lady, like all mystics, spoke in metaphors mere pedestrians could never understand. Everything they said always seemed to be above the heads of the masses. He understood that was why they always spoke on raised altars or lofty pulpits. Their words needed rarified air for transmission.

He figured that was why there was faith, to listen and act without having the vaguest idea why. She was just on a higher level of consciousness, and if he was to get there, too, he had to fall back on faith. Except for swallowing the four teeth, it hadn't failed him yet.

Again he asked, "Where do I find Hula Love?"

She didn't answer. Instead she began an ancient chant, threw her offering into the fiery caldera below, and sat stone quiet staring through the rain, something mystics seem to do better than most earthbounders. She had told him all he needed to know. So off he went, moving forward, listening to the inner voice and pausing frequently to drink water from the five-gallon silver and blue tank he cleverly integrated with his orange and brown deerskin backpack.

He was certain the Kahuna Lady had spoken the truth. Moving forward would keep him in the game. The twenty-two glasses of water kept his body free of germs, viruses, and other molecular invaders—probably drowned the hell out of them. He walked all over the five Hawaiian islands looking for Hula Love. A Filipino cane field worker under the big black cross in the middle of a sloping hilltop told him she had left on a big white boat, and pointed east over the Kunia Mountain Range toward the middle of North America. "She" had left. That's what he said. Now he was getting somewhere. Hula Love was a "she" not an it. Maybe the clouds were finally clearing.

So he took a big white boat, too, careful to avoid the sumptuous midnight buffets, karaoke contests, team-tag bingo tournaments and other tempting distractions that might dull his senses to the real mission. He did allow himself an hour a day to take private ballroom dancing lessons from the amply endowed dance instructor in the pink spandex pants and see-through tank top. The frequency of the lessons increased at about the same rate as their acrobatic trysts. The lust was delicious as usual and, as usual, left him with that same empty feeling when the marathon romps were over. He did what he always did, he worked out an erotic friendship agreement with her, and the lessons continued. Soon he was a recognized expert at every known dance and even invented a new one, the Mango Tango. It took the ship by storm. It started out with several sensual slow dips and turns interspersed with a few cheek-to-cheek bunny hops and a duck-walk pirouette. Depending on your blood alcohol level, some back-to-back tush rubbing and nose butting were optional moves. It was all in good fun and made people laugh, something dancing partners hadn't done in a long time. It also produced an unusually large number of marriage proposals and several sexual harassment suits.

Everybody wanted to learn the Mango Tango, so Bombay was kept busy day and night. He dropped another twenty-eight pounds, but it gave him an excellent opportunity to question many people.

Just about everyone had heard of Hula Love, but had no idea where to begin to look. Some had made feeble attempts but had wound up singing "Que Sera, Sera," and went back to their former routines. That was not an option for Bombay Curry. He had exhausted all the funds in his 401K program and figured if he didn't get a clue here in Martinique, he would be forced to spend the rest of his life on the island, listening, searching.

He walked up and down the rues Victor Hugo, Victor Severe, Republique, and back to Liberte, drinking water and listening.

A light warm rain started falling. He moved his face into the wind to catch the full brunt of the moisture. And that's when it happened.

The first sign. Maybe.

Silouetted against the white marble statue of Empress Josephine in La Savane Park was another over-sixty guy with a water tank, a backpack, and large brown bandages on his swollen shins. He was urinating against a giant black maplethorpe tree.

Is it possible he was not alone searching for Hula Love?

Before he could ask, the other guy smiled and said, "Yep, me too. Hell, there are thousands of us, maybe millions all over the planet walkin', drinkin', lookin'. You know, I bet if we all joined up we'd have a kinda network, you know, bigger than the Red Cross or the Holy Molies."

He had a kind round face and kept it alive with a big smile.

"I started eight years ago up in the Kenai peninsula in Alaska. Came darn close to finding her, but she slipped away." He unzipped his pants. "You'll have to excuse me, I'm up to thirty-four glasses a day." He moved to the other side of the maplethorpe and recycled his water, smiling all the time keeping his face turned to the wind.

"Tell me," Bombay asked, "what does she look like?"

"Wish I knew," he replied, "Everybody I've asked seemed to know who she is but had no idea what she looked like. Ain't that a pair of cotton socks?"

They became fast friends immediately, the way old men seem to do more easily than others. The rain and wind picked up a notch, so they moved to the leeward side of Josephine and continued to try to make sense of their nomadic search.

The New Friend took out a cellophane bag of Lilikoi pits and offered them to Bombay.

"Good for the circulation but don't bite down too hard."

"I know," Bombay said.

The New Friend extended his hand straight out to catch the rain. For no reason in particular, Bombay did the same thing. There they were, two displaced old geezers in a world they no longer understood smiling at the overflowing puddles of water streaming down their palms.

Suddenly the New Friend started laughing.

"Hey, pal, did you ever play mud football when you were a kid?"

"No, I was brought up in the city. We didn't have any mud."

"Whatdaysay we play us a game? Six points a touchdown, three touchdowns win."

"You're on."

They took off their shoes and socks, picked a particularly hard oval shaped breadfruit from a nearby tree, and started running, tackling, and falling face down in the thick layers of oozing black mud. Nobody scored any touchdowns. As a matter of fact, at some point they lost the breadfruit, but it didn't matter. They were kids again, invincible, no rules, just splashing, sloshing and sliding on a wet spongy magic carpet.

Soon they were covered head to toe in mud, and just lay there under the royal arm of Josephine laughing and inventing one funny exclamation after another just to let out the joy.

"Bazzomsooleeoolee." "Gafundziks." "Yeeeehooobulubulu." "Bulldickey boom boom."

Their laughter crackled through the empty park like summer thunder in a valley.

The sun broke through. They dried off, drank a few glasses of water, irrigated the turf around the maplethorpe, and leaned against the base of the statue.

The New Friend was still smiling, but he seemed to be getting older and older by the minute as he wrapped his swollen ankles.

"What's with the shins?" Bombay asked.

"Occupational injury. No big thing." The New Friend looked off the way people do when they hear something but aren't quite sure. He was speaking very slowly now.

"We're pretty lucky when you come to think about it," he mused.

"Whatdayamean?" Bombay replied.

"Well, because all of us over-sixty folks feel the same way at the same time in our history, I think that makes us the EDs."

"EDs?"

"Yeah, Evolutionary Drivers. You know, that part of the species out front who know everything is wrong and are looking for that one idea they can all agree on that takes them to the next step."

"I dunno. I think you're being too idealistic about how things change. The only real EDs in society are the warmongers and the real estate developers." Bombay said it, but his heart wasn't in it.

"Those folks only take over because we stop supporting ideas stronger than greed."

Bombay thought about that for a minute and offered, "You suppose Hula Love has the answer?"

"Hell, no. We already have all the answers."

Bombay was confused. "They why the hell are we walking around the world looking for her?"

"Because an answer isn't an answer until it touches the heart."

That came very close to being a metaphor, but left just enough room to be seen as a fact.

A light rain started falling again.

The New Friend started rubbing his chest slowly, methodically, the way cardiac patients always do. It never eases the pain within, but it helps fool the subconscious for a split second or two into believing you're still in control. He wasn't, but it didn't stop his thinking.

"You know, Bombay, it's a funny thing. When you know you're going to die soon it all becomes pretty clear. You just gotta get rid of all the myths, mysteries, and the old faiths and just kinda accept the real answers have been in your heart all along. I think, no, I'm sure, as soon as we left the birth canal we had everything we needed." A new burst of energy lit up his face and a deep, robust laugh racked his sagging body. "I guess that makes God just about the greatest comedy director of all time. Don't you see it? He creates existence, slaps some mud together, brings us on the scene, we look around and see we've got everything we need to survive, except *it*."

"*It?*"

"Yeah, you know, *it,* the thing we all want. But here's the comedy, we've already got *it,* inside, but we figure it's out there somewhere, so we spend the rest of our lives looking for what's under our noses all along. Much ado about nothing. The perfect comedy. You think maybe Shakespeare was God?" He attempted to slap Bombay on the back but his arm fell way short of the mark. "Can't you see it, Bombay? You have to let go of faith."

"Yeah, I can see it", Bombay answered," but I think you have to hang on to faith or there's no point in taking the next step."

The New Friend was rubbing his chest with more urgency as he barely made it to a nearby termite eaten wooden bench and sat down. His words were labored now, but just as clear as before.

"But that might be the point—let go of faith, keep on moving and listening, and what you may find will be greater than faith."

Bombay bent down, put his arm around the rain-soaked shivering New Friend and gently asked, "What could be greater than faith, my friend?"

His answer was immediate. "The truth. Sometimes faith just ends a search before it begins."

The rain fell much harder. The two friends sat in quiet for a long time, heads bent back letting the rain beat a steady refreshing tattoo on their faces. They giggled like little boys discovering their first summer swimming hole.

The New Friend was hunched over now in obvious pain, his arms dangling helplessly at his side. He muttered, "Do me a favor, willya, don't fuss about me when this thing is over. Let me be, and go find the Black Coral Lady at the Parc Floral et Culturel. She knows Hula Love."

His face lit up again with one of those big signature smiles as he whispered, "I sure could use a nice glass of cold water."

Before Bombay could fill his request, the New Friend closed his eyes and was gone. Bombay was moving now in a fast trot. Past the Hotel de Ville across the Place Jose-Marti to the great outdoor flower and fish market, Parc Floral et Culturel with the best of Martinique's exotic flora and gifts from the sea. He was impatient, more determined than at any time before on this confusing journey. He wouldn't accept mixed metaphors and stoic silences anymore. He wanted simple declarative answers and he wanted them right now.

His trot became a flat-out run. Large potted anthuriums, purple and orange bougainvillea, and fire opal heliconias swayed in his wake as he knifed through the enchanted marketplace scanning every face like a dying vulture in pursuit of his last meal.

He came to an abrupt stop where the philodendrons entwined with the papyrus ferns to form a lush trellis of green.

There she was sitting on a plain lahala mat with large chunks of gleaming black coral encircling her like adoring courtiers around a throne. A big, shiny ebony lady with a huge matronly bosom and the cold, steely confidence of one of those large frightening sopranos in a Wagnerian opera. She was covered with layers of silver chains and a black carnation lei. Her hair was criss-crossed with strands of beaded corn rows winding down around her shoulders and back up again. She didn't look up. And that was a good thing. Making eye contact with the Black Coral Lady would paralyze any pilgrim's ability to listen.

"Look, I need some straight answers—no mumbo jumbo about keeping the irrigation ditch full. My name is...."

"I know who you are and what you want." Unlike the Kahuna Lady, her words were course like shards of glass rattling in a wind tunnel. She had his attention. She continued, "May I please have a cold drink of water?"

She made a question sound like a Papal Bull.

Bombay poured a glass and handed it to her. She took it very gently like a geneticist examining a new strain of DNA. She drank slowly and then raised the glass skyward.

"It is the first and greatest satisfaction of all life," she said.

Oh brother, he thought, *here we go again with the Forrest Gump fortune cookie metaphors*. He was wrong. She was one of the New Paradigm Thinkers who used her words like a sawtooth tiger uses her chompers to bring down the weakest prey in the herd.

"There is no more eternal time. We're limited now, but we have the power to create our own future. This is the first age of the conscious evolution, and you are its champion. Accept it."

"What are you talking about lady? I'm just another self-medicating AARP card holder with high cholesterol and an enlarged prostate looking to bring back a little meaning, that's all."

The Black Coral Lady started shaking her head. The first signs of a grin appeared. Bombay had had it. His anger and frustration lit a great fire. He was pacing up and down, slamming his fist into his other open hand, the gift of tongues was upon him and the whole marketplace became a rapt congregation. He continued in a loud, pleading voice. "I just want to believe things are going to get better. I want things to be simple again, nobody put on hold, doctors who make house calls, foul lines with consequences. Music that doesn't sound like puking to a beat. God, I miss Benny Goodman. Whatdahell is going on? Where did this empty new world come from? I didn't make it. Don't look at me. I did my homework. I played by the rules and cared about things, and what do I have to show for it? Part-time work as a greeter at Walmart, Windows 98, and the goddamn Home Shopping Network. It's not enough!" He turned abruptly and moved menacingly toward the Black Coral Lady. His permanently frozen right index finger inches away from her massive flaring nostrils.

"If you've got a message for me, lady, now is the time to deliver it. Direct and to the point, if you please."

She was, kinda. Each word a thunderbolt, sharp, intense, unequivocal, at least as far as she was concerned. "Go back," she said, "and find that moment when everything worked. Hula Love will be there. Then evolve to a better place. The world will follow you. Unitas chose you to carry the E-link because this next turn of the species is too important to be left to the Holy Molies and Informercial Brooks Brothers Gurus. Every leader has failed us because they've taken the Soul out of their message. If a commoner can't find Hula Love, then nobody can, and we've lost our last chance."

Bombay knew there was no use debating this absurdity.

"Okay, right, lady. I'm the man out front. I've got the big E on my chest. So how about a little hint. How do I find Hula Love and turn things around? And don't tell me to listen to the little voice within. I've been listening halfway around the world. I'm broke, soaking wet, my bladder is the size of Hoover Dam, and I'm looking at spending the rest of my life on the dole in the middle of the Caribbean."

The entire congregation leaned forward. This was the moment of truth for all searchers.

The Black Coral Lady did what all Mountaintoppers do when they deliver the big answer, she paused. Finally, she took out an old gray cloth and started polishing a piece of coral. When she was convinced her work was complete, she bellowed, "Can you dance?"

Bombay was too tired to resist anymore, "Yeah, I dance. Swing, jazz, ballroom, salsa, you name it, anything but the Macarena. I hate that crap."

"You any good?" she shot back.

"I invented the Mango Tango, but what has this got to do with anything?"

She lowered her head and said quietly, "That's your answer."

She handed him a large chunk of coral and went inside herself to another place. Bombay slowly made his way back to the seawall, dejected, confused, convinced he was the only being left alive who didn't speak in parabolic metaphors. He felt something else—the end of hope. He bought a Creole Lady pin cushion with his last five dollars, and sat there staring at the Millennium Clock until sunset. A loud blast of the big white boat's whistle summoned all her passengers back onboard. Bombay figured he's get his clothes out of his cabin, come back to the seawall, and spend the rest of his life on an island half the size of Jersey City looking for Hula Love.

It didn't work out like that.

When he reached the gangway, the cruise director, a store front mannequin with a plastic smile surgically implanted behind his nose, was anxiously waving his arms, pointing at Bombay.

"You're the father of the Mango Tango, right?"

"Yeah, right. Why?"

"Today is your lucky day. I just found out one of our Gentleman Dance Hosts passed away suddenly. He just sat down on a park bench and died. How would you like to take his place?"

So Bombay Curry spent the next nine-and-a-half years cruising around the world doing the Mango Tango with single old ladies in comfortable shoes and talcum powder stains on their black dresses. He found no joy in this work, but loved the opportunity to walk up to the forecastle in rough weather and catch the ocean spray on his face.

He searched for Hula Love in every deep water port on the globe. He went inland to the foot of the Himalayas, up the Lualaba to the headwaters of the Congo, on top of Machu Picchu, and across the Sinai twice. He followed every lead. He heard a thousand sincere explanations of who or what Hula Love was. Each raised his consciousness just a little higher while lowering his expectations just as much. He listened to them all—poets, Mindbenders, Holy Molies, bartenders, and once, after indulging himself with a hydrocolon cleansing in a natural herb health club in Bangkok, a lady in a green silk kimono who had almost convinced him Hula Love was in the Federal Witness Protection Program in Buffalo, New York.

He was growing very tired. Then one day while doing the Mango Tango line dance with fourteen great-grandmothers from Tupelo Mississippi, he suddenly remembered the words of the Black Coral Lady, "Go back and find the moment when everything worked…and you'll find Hula Love." So he spent hours sitting in the sun looking down at the wake of the ship going over every positive memory he'd ever had. Defective sun block caused severe second degree burns and forced him indoors where he temporarily lost the will to search the past.

The feared deadline for disaster came and went. Day one of the new Millennium dawned, and no major doomsday event rocked the world. But Armageddon, like all transformations, starts in small disguised ways. There were definite signs: public access TV had edged out reality shows for the highest ratings; every one on the planet except a small group of survivalists in Missoula, Montana, had his own web site and was selling something to someone else; the Chambers of Commerce in Maine and Vermont had steadfastly refused to believe it was global warming that had plunged their states into subtropical temperatures all year round, and were mounting ad campaigns to replace the Bahamas as the number one winter vacation destination on the east coast.

Wearing a large sombrero and super-sun block 34, Bombay was back looking down at the wake of the ship. He thought, "Maybe Hula Love isn't the answer. Maybe she never existed in the first place. Maybe she was just a giant cosmic carrot on a string, a universal dream that keeps the species moving forward before the inevitable final fall. Maybe The New Friend was right. Life was nothing more than a giant long-running sitcom."

Still, there was a little place inside him that hoped she was real, but the light was fading.

Boredom and arthritic shin bones brought about by constant banging from inept dance partners ended his life at sea.

He wound up where all searchers end up, at the beginning. He disembarked in Honolulu, Hawaii, with a small brown suitcase, a large chunk of black coral, and a limp. He rented a small room above the old Beachboy Bar and Grill at the harbor across from the Aloha Tower. Along with the old Moana Hotel, they were about the only island landmarks that remained from the romantic days of the last century. He spent his time rummaging through nostalgia shops and volunteering at the Neptune Society making sure the labels on the small boxes of ashes matched the true identity of the occupant. He was pretty good at it until failing eyesight caused a grieving Pakistani Hindu family to scatter the ashes of a teacup Chihuahua named Pancho Chico under the mistaken belief it was their uncle Haseem Rajah. It probably made no difference in the long run because most families, with the exception of the Musuba Matinkers in Northern Borneo, can see any resemblance of their loved one in a pile of ash, but his old Catholic guilt was still hanging around, and he quit.

He started rubbing his chest a lot in the fall of 2010, but kept moving forward. He no longer carried his own water tank, so he had to carefully plan his days to always be within a few hundred feet of a drinking fountain.

Then one day in late April a strange thing happened that forever changed Bombay Curry's life and, perhaps, sealed the fate of his species.

He was sneezing repeatedly from all the dust covering the old posters in the basement of *Waikiki Memories*, the last nostalgia shop within walking distance of his room. The fog of old age had pretty much erased his past, so he wasn't sure why he was still searching or what he was looking for. He didn't even remember he was carrying around the E-link cipher and was supposed to save the world. All he knew was that he had found no answers that satisfied him, so here he was, in the only place that gave him some consolation, back where he started. He smiled at all the faded brown sepia posters and their gushy art deco depiction of the lei-decked romantic couples holding hands on an idyllic white sandy beach as the sun set over an unobstructed view of Diamond Head. It was real and unreal at the same time. He was talking to himself now.

"That's what I always wanted. I think, no, I'm sure, that's what we've always wanted. A love that always seems to be this young, this committed, where everything is prologue but, hey, it only exists on dusty old posters, my friend."

He continued sneezing and thumbing through the pile. He came to the last poster dated, Saturday, April 30, 1939. "Funny," he mumbled, "today is Saturday, April 30." The proprietor, another very old man, drinking a large glass of water, overheard him and offered the explanation. "That's because 1939 and 2010 have the same calendar dates. Happens once every hundred years."

Bombay looked back at the poster, an advertisement for a very special event way back when. As he adjusted his thick glasses with the reinforced steel rims and read the words under the picture his face lit up. He knew the journey was either over or about to begin.

It was the most perfect night in a history of perfect nights. The buzz of a hundred happy conversations was humming with a new excitement. The colorful Saturday night dance crowd at the fabled Moana Hotel knew they were making history. The dreamlike outdoor garden ballroom with the giant Ainahau banyan tree in the center where Robert Louis Stevenson read his tales of the South Pacific to the young legendary beauty, Princess Ka'iulani, was hosting a new radio show that would send Hawaii's special message of Aloha to the mainland for the first time. Ladies in bright multi-colored floral print dresses and sweet smelling maile leis swirled like giddy nymphs at a celestial feast in the arms of their smiling partners. Pua Almeida and His Happy Hawaiian Serenaders, framed on stage in a giant wreath of white ginger blossoms, were playing a soft, haunting rendition of *The King Kamehameha Waltz*.

The unmistakable romantic twang of a half dozen steel guitars melted into the beat of the Pacific, a few yards away, pounding the coral heads and reflecting silver moonbeams up and down Waikiki Beach.

A light trade wind sweeping down from the Koolaus carried the breath of a thousand tropical flowers along with a light mist, more refreshing than annoying. Bombay moved his face into the wind to catch the warm moisture. He was in another time and had no idea how he got here, nor did he care. If idylls become real for just one moment in a life, then this was it. If a rhapsody had more than music, if it had color, contentment, laughter and love, then it was surely playing now. Not one false beat. Could this be the happiest place in the galaxy? Everything was working. All senses were complete. He was young again and all things were possible. If he could be anything, do anything that would make a difference, it would be now.

The silver haired emcee in the white dinner jacket and red bow tie took a cue from the engineer, covered his ear with one hand and spoke into the large boxed microphone.

"Alooooha from paradise. Here on the white glittering sands of Waikiki, Hawaii callssss."

His rich soothing baritone resonated like a siren's whisper up and down the shoreline, up the rich green slopes of Diamond Head, and then out over the glistening Pacific.

A stunningly elegant dark-skinned young island girl in a red lava glow muu muu and a fresh hibiscus in her hair walked on stage. The crowd broke out into enthusiastic applause. The Happy Hawaiians began moving their fingers over the taunt strings of their steel guitars.

"Ladies and gentlemen," the emcee continued, "we've asked Hawaii's first lady of music to open this historic broadcast with a new song of the islands written especially for this moment. One we know is destined to capture hearts everywhere with the magic and meaning of Aloha. Miss Genoa Keawe singing 'Hula Love.'" Her lilting falsetto glided over the lyrics like a soft breeze moving through velvet. They spoke of a love that frees the heart to see all life as one, a love that builds with each sharing, ultimately changing the world, a love that lives in every heart but is found by very few.

Bombay had heard these thoughts before. They weren't new, but answers aren't answers until they touch the heart.

He took a sip of his pineapple passion fruit drink, inhaled deeply, and looked up through the blue mist at the oddly shaped oval moon.

"It's a kapakahi moon," the lady with the gleaming black coral hair said.

"Kapakahi?" he repeated.

"Yes, it means strange angles. Happens only once every hundred years. We call it a papaya moon."

Bombay turned and looked at her for the first time. Their hearts smiled before they did. She took off her kukui nut lei and placed it around Bombay's neck. Her words were soft like the old Kahuna Lady. "Kukui Pio'ole. The oil from the kukui nut was used as a source of fuel for torch lighting in ancient times. Now it symbolizes the light, the guide."

As a marker of historical time, April 30, 1939, was memorable for three events. The greatest exhibition of the future ever held, the World's Fair, opened on a former sheep meadow in Flushing, New York. The sign over the entrance both greeted and warned all visitors, *The world is poised on the brink of a new future. For good or ill, it will be up to each one of you to decide.*

The second event escaped everyone's notice until many years later. An Eskimo named Hamshok Ibee in a tiny fishing village in northwest Greenland invented the first bottled water. He also patented a device that would allow you to carry it with you everywhere you went. The tribal medicine man proclaimed it the greatest invention of the century and would improve the health of the universe beyond imagination.

And the third—a major eruption on the sun caused a shower of solar flares. They disrupted world-wide radio transmissions and allowed a local Hawaiian radio broadcast calculated to reach only as far as Fresno, California, to be heard by millions of people in every corner of seven continents including the northwest corner of Greenland.

Audio physicists say it is a rare phenomena in the atmosphere called *unitas,* an unexplained condition which causes air waves to transcend their normal frequencies and be picked up in every area of the globe and beyond.

It is said to happen once every hundred years.

They looked at the moon for a very long time, held hands, and won first place in the dance contest. It was something never seen before in the islands. It started out with several sensual slow dips and turns interspersed with a few cheek-to-cheek bunny hops and a duck-walk pirouette.

Bombay Curry and the lady in the gleaming black coral hair walked for hours under the blue papaya moon. They only spoke once. "Wouldn't it be a wonderful gift to the future," she said, "if somehow every heart in the universe could be with us here tonight in this beautiful dream we call Hawaii and be touched by the power of Hula Love?"

"I wish I could make it happen," he replied. Bombay leaned back and looked up at the blue ceiling of stars above him. He slowly reached up to touch one.

0-595-33557-8